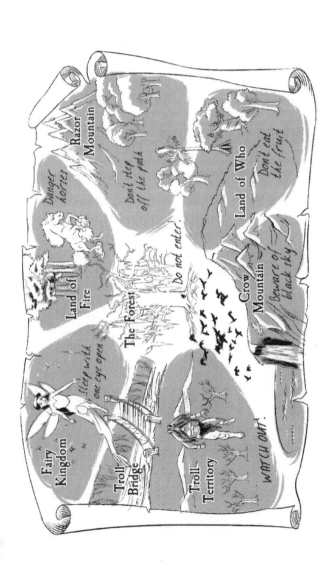

Other Books by Terry Nolan

Elm Underwood Series
Forbidden Forest
A Murder of Crows

Forbidden Forest

Terry Nolan
Copyright 2020

Printed by Kindle Publishing

This is a work of fiction. Names, characters, organizations, places, events and incidents are either products of the author's imagination or are used fictitiously. Any resemblance to actual person, living or dead, or actual events is purely coincidental.

Cover design Ghislain Viau
Creative Publishing Book Design

ISBN 978-1-7348533-0-8
e-book 978-1-7348533-1-5

Dedication

To my grandsons, Josh and Zac,
and to my sister, Faye. She believed in me,
and gave her support and encouragement.

ACKNOWLEDGEMENTS

Thanks to my editor Staci Mauney with Prestige Prose

Thanks to Ghislain Vaiu with Creative Publishing Book Design for the book cover and map design.

Thanks to Creel McFarland with Limerick Studios for my photo.

Thanks to Mary Wagoner, a friend, a neighbor and most importantly a teacher. She assisted in proofreading the manuscript one more time before submission to the publisher.

My fellow critique group members for their support and encouragement. They were very patient, and helpful with my deep learning curve on how to write. Thanks to Dave, Cindy, Sue, and Dick.

Thanks to all my co-workers at Patti's Hallmark for constantly listening to me chattered about all the characters and what they were up to. I know they wondered if I would ever finish the book and get it published.

Thanks to the two young boys that live near me, Jacob and Kason. They offered several great ideas for the book. Sorry they were not used in this book, but may be used in the future.

Forbidden Forest

Asher

Hope you enjoy the adventure

Terry

Table of Contents

Chapter 1	The Forest	1
Chapter 2	Moving Day	8
Chapter 3	Spying	11
Chapter 4	The Neighbors	15
Chapter 5	Grandpa's Stories	23
Chapter 6	Into the Forest	32
Chapter 7	Beneath the Tree	39
Chapter 8	A New World	45
Chapter 9	First Night	53
Chapter 10	Fight or Flight	64
Chapter 11	Fairy Help	69
Chapter 12	Badlands	77
Chapter 13	A Rescue	82
Chapter 14	Unexpected Help	89
Chapter 15	Together Again	97
Chapter 16	Training	101
Chapter 17	Birds, Bats, and Snakes, Oh No	106
Chapter 18	Etchings on the Wall	115
Chapter 19	Who Are You	121
Chapter 20	Trees	126
Chapter 21	Home	136

Chapter 1

The Forest

"I'm going out," Elm yelled as he grabbed his backpack and opened the back door, then whispered, "into the woods."

He adjusted his baseball cap. It was white with the letter H embroidered in black. The H stood for the middle school mascot, a hawk. Elm owned dozens of caps in different colors, all with either the letter H or a white hawk.

"Don't go out of the yard." His mom's voice carried through an open window.

His parents constantly reminded him and his sister, Willow, not to go into the forest. Why did their parents live in a house next to dangerous woods? It didn't make any sense to his eleven-year-old mind.

Elm looked back to make sure no one was watching him as he hurried into a small patch of trees, where his dad had built a treehouse. It was still part of the backyard. Sequoia, his dog raced after him. The dog leaped up, slamming into his back. Elm stumbled and raised his arms to keep from crashing face first on the ground. He rolled over and laughed as his dog licked his face while wagging his tail.

"Sequoia, stop it. Are you going with me?" The dog whined and blocked the pathway. Again, he glanced at the house. The
sunshine against the tin roof bounced into his eyes, blinding him. He pulled the bill of his cap down, then turned toward the forest, spots dancing in front of his eyes. He rubbed his eyes and took several steps. Again, the dog growled and sat on the path.

Elm heard his mom's words as if she stood right beside him. He repeated them to the dog as he continued to walk. "I know what mom says. 'Elm, don't play in the woods unless your sister is with you.' 'Elm, don't go past the fence posts into the forest.' Give me a break! She acts like I'm a baby. And why are there fence posts and no fence? If the forest is dangerous, why no fence to separate it from the house? How can I stay out of the woods when the whole farm is covered in trees?"

Elm's dad, an arborist, owned a nursery in town. The trees he sold grew on their ten-acre farm. His dad told him if he listened, the trees would whisper his name. No matter how quietly he sat under the trees, which was very hard for Elm to do, he never heard the trees say anything.

His dad also warned him and his sister not to explore the forest. He said the thick undergrowth caused people to become confused and lose their way.

Elm walked past the wooden posts and into the forest. The skin on the back of his neck prickled as the dog whined beside him. This wasn't the first time he'd crossed the boundary line. Of course, any time you're told not to do something, you have to try it at least once or twice. This was his third time. Each time he ventured a little farther into the forest, always carrying his backpack. He never knew what he might find. On his first trip, he found a child's miniature car, which was now in his pack.

"Are you a scaredy-cat? Do you think there are monsters in the woods?" Elm glanced at the dog.

As fallen leaves crackled under Elm's feet, Sequoia followed with his nose to the ground. Off to the sides of the path, vines crept up tree trunks, and dense undergrowth covered the ground. Damp earth filled Elm's nostrils. A light breeze rustled the leaves above causing shadows to dance across the trail. As he glanced from side to side, beads of sweat dripped down his cheeks. He stood still for only a moment, then took several more steps. He wanted to prove to himself that he could walk through the woods without getting lost.

He passed a rotten log. The same one he had seen on his last trip. The one he could see from his treehouse. It sometimes glowed with bluish-green lights. His dad called it a foxfire also known as fairy fire. Elm never saw any fairies, just plenty of fireflies.

Hearing twigs breaking in the distance, he turned to Sequoia. "Did you hear that? Willow, are you following me?" He expected his twelve-year-old sister to jump out in front of him. He removed his cap and ran his hands through his hair as a giggle slipped out of his mouth. "Willow, I know you're there." He squinted through the bushes but didn't see anyone.

The dog's ears lay back, and he tucked his tail between his legs. Elm scratched the dog behind his ear. "It's only squirrels. Let's keep going."

They continued in silence, listening to the leaves rustling all around them. Elm wished he had brought a long rope to mark his path to ensure he didn't get lost.

He passed the point of his last trip, but before continuing, he pulled a compass from his backpack to check the direction. He was headed east. Slowly, he moved farther into the forest. The trees along the path grew so close together, they created a wall and blocked the sun. The path darkened. Elm hesitated a moment, but curiosity compelled him to continue. No birds sang in the trees, and silence surrounded him.

"Next time, I'll bring a flashlight and a rope," he said out loud.

Just a little farther. If he stayed too long, his mom would realize he wasn't in the yard.

He crept around a sharp bend. Stopping, his mouth fell open and his eyes widened. The sun's rays bounced off the dew-filled leaves and sparkled against something on the ground. He bent over and picked up a child's whistle. *How did this get here?* He put it in his backpack. Standing up, he saw an enormous tree in the middle of a clearing. He raised his chin higher, but he couldn't see the top of the tree. Sequoia growled as his hackles raised.

"Calm down," Elm said. "Holy smokes, it must be hundreds of years old." He stared at an ancient live oak tree covered in Spanish moss.

Nothing unusual about live oak trees. They grew all around town. But this tree was different. It stood taller than the other trees in the forest. Its upper branches reached high into the sky while the lower ones reached a great distance, as if to keep anything from growing near it. Its roots spread across the ground like a nest of snakes ready to strike. Wisps of air blew through the moss causing it to stretch toward him, like bony fingers reaching for his skin. He backed up a couple of steps.

"Come closer, young Elm. I've been waiting for you."

"Who said that?" Elm's head whipped around as his heart tried to claw its way out of his chest. The roots of the oak moved. Sequoia whimpered and pawed at Elm's pant leg.

"Come closer," a voice murmured.

With a sense of foreboding, Elm's eyes narrowed as he stared at the oak tree. "Did you say that?"

"Closer."

Elm whirled around and stumbled over several roots, landing face down. Roots slithered around his ankle. The rough wood scratched his skin. It dragged him toward a small hole at the base of the tree until Sequoia chomped down on the root, causing it to loosen its grip.

Elm unraveled the root from his leg, jumped up, and rushed back to the path with Sequoia beside him. He stared at the tree. Everything seemed normal. Did he trip and get tangled in the roots? Did he imagine the roots dragging him? He reached up and touched his cap. Knowing the hawk mascot was with him gave him a little courage. He reached over his shoulder and touched his backpack, then whispered to his dog, "Let's go home." For some unknown reason, he didn't want the live oak tree to hear him.

5

Dark clouds filled the sky above the trees, blocking the sun. Darkness followed him as he raced down the path. Once the oak tree was out of sight, Elm checked his compass. The needle spun out of control.

"Sequoia, which way?"

The dog barked and led him down the trail. Elm noticed a folded paper on the trail that hadn't been there earlier. He stooped down and picked it up, then stuffed it in his backpack. He would check it out once he was out of the forest.

When Elm saw the fence posts, he sprinted until he reached them. Winded, he stopped to catch his breath, while Sequoia continued toward the house.

"Where have you been?" Willow stood a few feet away from him.

Startled, he jumped. "None of your business."

"You know you're not supposed to go in the forest." Willow placed her hands on her hips.

"I wasn't alone. Sequoia went with me. Stop acting like Mom. You're only thirteen months older than me. That doesn't make you in charge."

He watched Willow turn back to the house. She crossed her arms and let out a "humph."

"Wait," Elm said. "Have you ever gone past the fence post?"

She smiled. "Yes, but just a short distance. I felt like someone was watching me, so I came back to the yard."

"We need to go together. I have to show you something," Elm said.

"What?"

"I'm not going to say. You have to see it."

"Now?" Willow asked.

"No, another day."

"Maybe," she mumbled as she glanced toward the forest.

"Have you ever heard the trees talk?" Elm asked.

She stayed silent for a moment. "I've heard...I thought I heard a voice once."

"While in the forest?"

"Yes, that's why I never went back."

"Have you told anyone?" Elm asked.

Willow tilted her head to the side. "What? And have people think I'm crazy?"

"No, not people. Have you told Mom or Dad?"

"No," she said.

"Okay, I won't either. Let's go in the house." He glanced up. The sky was clear blue with no clouds. Had it been his imagination? Trees don't talk, or do they? As he headed to the back door, the sensation of being watched caused him to dash into the house.

Chapter 2

Moving Day

The next morning, Elm heard the roar of a truck. It reminded him of a nightmare. Something about a tree, danger, and...something he couldn't quite remember. A loud banging noise drew his attention to the window. He rushed over and peered out. Turning around, he bumped into a chair, knocking it over. Ignoring the fallen chair, he rushed down the steps.

Willow, not far behind him, stopped at the kitchen door. "What's going on? Why are you still in your pajamas?" She placed her hands over her nose and mouth and backed away. "Are you sick? Stay away from me! I don't want to get sick over the weekend."

Elm ignored her. "Mom! Dad!" He cried. "Someone is moving into the house next door. I saw people carrying boxes into it."

"New neighbors!" Willow rushed into the kitchen, her red curly hair bouncing against her shoulders. "I hope they have a girl my age and no boys! Can we go see?"

Elm stuck out his tongue at his sister, then faced his dad. "Do you know who they are?"

A few seconds passed as they waited for him to respond, then he said, "I didn't know the farm next door was for sale. I remember the previous owners, the Millers. I wonder what happened to them."

His dad stared out the window, lost in thought. Elm jerked on his sleeve. "Dad! When can we meet the new neighbors?"

"Let's give them time to unpack. We'll go over tomorrow after lunch, introduce ourselves, and offer our help," Dad replied.

Elm agreed.

"Go upstairs and get dressed. You have twenty minutes before the school bus arrives," Mom said.

Back in his room, Elm gazed out the window and watched the activities. Excited about a new neighbor and maybe a boy his age, he forgot about the live oak tree in the forest.

His mom yelled, "Elm, you're going to be late. It's time for the bus."

He dressed, grabbed a blue cap, then sprinted through the kitchen. He took a piece of toast on his way out the door. His backpack bumped against him as he jogged to the end of the driveway.

"Do you remember the Millers?" Elm asked.

"Sure, it wasn't that long ago that they lived next door. Jacob was five years old. He liked to sneak into our backyard to play with the dog. He called him C.Q. instead of Sequoia." Willow laughed.

"Do you think they just disappeared?"

She sniggered. "Really? You think, poof, and the family was gone?"

"No. What if they went into the forest and got lost?"

"That's a terrible thing to say. What is it with you and the woods?" Willow winced.

Elm reached into his backpack. "I found this in the forest. It's a child's whistle."

"I don't want to talk about this. It frightens me to think they're wandering around in the forest." Willow shuddered.

Elm put the whistle back and started to pull out the folded paper, but the bus drove up and he decided to wait. Elm continued to think about the Millers, the forest, and the tree roots dragging him toward a hole in the tree.

Chapter 3

Spying

Saturday morning, Elm woke before anyone else. He couldn't wait to find out if the new family had children. He peered out his window but didn't see anyone.

"C'mon, Sequoia, let's go out." He tiptoed down the steps, careful not to make any noise.

"Let's play ball," he said to the dog. He picked up the ragged tennis ball and tossed it toward the neighbor's house. Sequoia jumped in the air, catching it, and brought it back to Elm.

"This is not getting me any closer," he said out loud. This time he flung the ball, and it landed in some bushes. Sequoia, unable to retrieve it, sat down.

Elm smiled. "Oh, sorry, boy."

He shoved his hands into the bush. Instead of reaching for the ball, he moved some small branches and craned forward for a better view of the house next door. His heart pounded in his ears so hard, he didn't hear his sister sneak up behind him.

Willow leaned over, and in a loud voice asked, "What are you doing? Spying?"

Elm almost jumped out of his skin. He turned and watched Willow race toward the house. When she reached the back door, she turned and yelled, "Elm! Mom said it's time for breakfast."

He rushed through the kitchen door letting it slam behind him. Trying to catch his breath, he said, "Mom, she was spying on me."

"What? What were you doing?" His mom frowned.

"Nothing." He sat down and glared at his sister across the table.

She mouthed the word, "Idiot."

"That's enough, Willow." Her mom turned just in time to catch her.

Willow muttered under her breath.

After breakfast, Elm wandered outside, curious to find out about the neighbors. He decided to climb an apple tree for a better view of the house next door. Under the tree, he jumped and grabbed a sturdy branch. Pulling himself up, an apple pelted him in the head.

"Ow! Who's doing that?"

He covered his head with his hands, then twisted around, expecting to see Willow, but he was all alone. He shaded his eyes and stared up into the tree. A few more apples fell on him.

"Okay, I'm not going to climb you."

To his surprise, the apples stopped falling. Bewildered, he shook his head as he moved away from the tree. He glanced back to see if any more apples fell. No, not a one.

He proceeded to the next tree, a large weeping willow with sturdy branches. He scrambled up ten feet without a problem, even though the overnight dew made the limbs slippery. He settled into a Y-shaped branch, perfect for sitting. He wished he'd brought his binoculars.

Unable to see the house next door, Elm climbed farther out on the limb. Still unable to see, he parted a few smaller branches. Glancing back at the neighbor's, he saw someone was staring at him through a window. Suddenly, the blinds closed. He sucked in his breath, scooted backward, and lost his balance. Grasping for the branch, he plummeted.

His stomach lurched. He closed his eyes and gritted his teeth, bracing for impact. But instead of slamming into the ground, something curled around his body, slowing his descent and placing him gently on the ground.

He watched as flexible willow branches drew away from his body, returning to hang like normal. He blinked.

Wide-eyed, he asked, "What the heck?"

He jumped up and bolted to the house. Something very strange was happening with the trees.

As he stepped onto the back porch, the aroma of fresh-baked chocolate cookies filled the air, calming his nerves.

"Are you okay? You look a little pale," his mom said.

"I'm fine." He glanced out the back door toward the tree, then turned back to his mom. "I hope you made enough cookies for us and the neighbors."

With a laugh, she said, "You're just like your dad, always thinking about your stomach." She walked to the bottom of the stairs and yelled, "Willow, hurry up."

Elm smiled. Time to find out who or what was next door. *What was next door? Why would I think that?* He forgot about the willow tree's strange behavior in his excitement to meet the neighbors.

Chapter 4

The Neighbors

Elm watched his mom place the cookies on a plate while Willow arranged fresh flowers in a vase to take to the neighbors. *Finally*. Elm hurried ahead of everyone and pressed the doorbell.

A woman with long, black hair opened the door, holding a baby in her arms.

"We don't want to interrupt, but we thought we'd drop by to say welcome to the neighborhood," Dad said.

"Oh, are you from next door?" the woman asked.

"Yes, we're the Underwoods," Mom replied. "I'm Kai, and this is my husband Adare."

"Come in. Please don't pay any attention to the mess." The lady led them into the living room. Boxes sat on top of each other at odd angles ready to tumble at any moment.

"Who is this green-eyed beauty with the flowers?" the lady asked.

Willow giggled. "I'm Willow. These are from our garden. I picked them this morning."

Tired of waiting, Elm blurted, "I'm Elm. Do you have any kids? I mean, besides the baby."

"Elm!" Dad said.

"Yes," she replied, then looked at Mom. "I'm Tala, and this is Bella. She's seven months old."

Willow placed the flowers and cookies on a study looking box.

A man with a dark beard and mustache entered the living room.

"Lance, these are our neighbors, Adare, Kai, Willow, and Elm."

"Willow and Elm?" Lance raised an eyebrow. "Your family has an affinity for trees."

"Yeah," Dad said, as he shook Lance's hand. "It's a family tradition."

"We're the Wolffs, and when there's a full moon, you better watch out." Lance smiled showing his teeth.

Elm and Willow exchanged a glance. Even though the man's teeth looked normal, they took a step back.

"Oh, honey, stop it," Mrs. Wolff said. "He's only teasing. He loves to joke about our name."

Lance moved to the wide staircase. "Randy, come down and meet the neighbors."

Elm saw a boy about his age come down the steps. When he reached the bottom step, he leaped off onto the floor. He had dark, wavy hair and a crooked smile.

"Randy, this is Mr. and Mrs. Underwood. And these two are their trees... um, kids...Elm and Willow," Lance said.

"Hey," Randy said as he glanced from one to the other.

"Hey," Elm replied. "You wanna come over to our house?"

Randy nodded, then faced his dad.

"You may go. Be back in one hour. You have lots of chores to do."

Willow twirled her hair around her finger as she said, "If you ever need a babysitter, I'll be glad to help."

"I usually do the babysitting." Randy moved closer to his sister in a protective manner.

A little flustered, Willow's cheeks turned as red as her hair. "Maybe we can babysit together." She pivoted and rushed out the door. The adults chuckled.

"Come on, let's go," Elm mumbled. "Sisters can be so silly. Do you have any brothers or sisters besides the baby?"

"No, just Bella and me," Randy replied.

As they walked past Elm's house, he said, "Wait a sec." He rushed over to the back porch and picked up his backpack.

17

"Cool backpack, why does it have a white hawk on it?" Randy asked.

"The white hawk is the middle school mascot. It represents strength and courage. The *H* on my cap also stands for the hawk," Elm said.

"Are you in middle school?" Randy asked.

"No. Not yet, but next year," Elm said. "I mean, next school year. Are you?"

"I'll start middle school next year too," Randy replied.

When they caught up with Willow, she said, "Your dad's kinda funny."

"No, he isn't. He thinks he is, but he's just embarrassing."

"Aren't all parents?" Elm laughed.

They walked a short distance into the trees behind their home and approached a clump of pine trees. Attached to one of the trees stood a ten-foot, homemade ladder which led to a treehouse. Not quite a treehouse, it didn't have a roof.

"Let's go up," Elm said. "This is our place where no parents are allowed."

"This is cool," Randy said in amazement as he looked around at the backyard and then out into the forest.

Sitting on the floor of the treehouse, Elm asked, "How old are you?"

"I'll be twelve in October."

"Me too. When in October? Mine's the twenty-ninth, almost Halloween. I usually have a wicked party." Elm laughed at his own joke. "Get it? Halloween, wicked party."

Randy snickered. "The thirteenth. I was born on a Friday, and this year my birthday falls on Friday, the thirteenth." Randy glanced at Willow. "When's yours?"

"September first. I'll be thirteen," Willow said.

"So, what's there to do around here?" Randy asked.

"We ride our bikes to town and visit our grandpa or go to the park or the movies," Elm said.

"You're allowed to ride your bikes on the main road?"

"Sure. Do you have a bike?" Elm asked.

"Yes," Randy replied.

"Great, we'll show you around town sometime, and while we're at it, we'll stop and visit with our grandpa. He lives in town," Elm said.

"We also ride to the lake to go swimming," Willow added.

"Whoa, you swim in a lake?" Randy glanced from Elm to Willow. "I've only swum in a pool."

"We'll take you, and I'm sure you'll love it," Willow said.

"We climb lots of trees," Elm said.

"Didn't I see you in the willow tree looking at our house?" Randy glanced at Elm.

Elm lowered his head as his cheeks turned red. "Yeah, I wanted to know if any kids lived there." Changing the subject, he stood up. "Look over there."

Randy stood and eyed the area where Elm was pointing.

"Can you see the fence post?"

"Yeah."

"We're not allowed to go into the forest past the post. It's mostly a tangle of underbrush, and our dad says it's easy to get lost. I thought I'd let you know in case you decide to play back here when we're not around."

"Grandpa calls it our enchanted forest," Willow said.

Randy arched his eyebrows. "Why? Is it haunted?"

"No, just Grandpa being silly," Elm said. "I want to show you what I found the other day when I went into the forest."

"I thought you just said you weren't allowed in the forest," Randy said.

"We're not, but I did, and I found..."

Mr. Underwood called from the back porch, interrupting their conversation. "Randy, it's time to go home. We don't want you in trouble on your first visit."

"Thanks," Randy replied. "I've gotta finish unpacking and setting up my room. I'll see you later." He scrambled down the ladder and rushed toward his house.

Elm and Willow walked toward the house.

Elm said, "I need to tell you..."

Their mom opened the kitchen door. "Well, what do you think of Randy?".

"I like him," Elm replied.

"Me too." Willow giggled.

"That was obvious!" Elm said. "Oh, Randy, maybe someday we can babysit together. Yuck!"

"Okay, you two, enough!"

Elm turned and went to his room. He pulled the paper from his pack. It was old and brittle and smelled musty. He carefully unfolded it. His mouth dropped open. It was a treasure map. No, not treasure, but a map of some kind. It was divided into several different regions. In tiny print, each region had a warning. Across the top of the map it stated, Don't Enter the Forest. Elm snickered. *Too late for that warning.* In the middle of the map stood the enormous live oak tree. A path wound from the tree in a circle that spread farther and farther away from the tree but eventually led back and ended near it.

His pulse raced. He knocked on Willow's door. When she stuck her head out of her room, he opened his mouth, but no words came out. His throat was dry. He held up one finger, then ran to the bathroom to swallow some water. He rushed back and said, "Hurry! See what I found."

"Pee-yew, that smells. Did you draw it?" Willow pinched her nose closed.

"No." He shifted from one foot to the other. "I found it the other day when I was in the woods. We need to follow it and see where it goes."

Gaping at him, she opened her mouth then closed it. "No." She put her hand out. "Let me see it."

"No, you'll tear it up. And don't go telling Mom or Dad."

Willow glanced at the map. "Don't do anything stupid until I've had time to think about it."

Elm folded up the map and placed it back into his pack. Sooner or later, he would go back into the forest.

Chapter 5

Grandpa's Stories

Several weeks passed, and Elm didn't mention the map again. But he looked at it every day and wondered why it had been in the woods.

Willow knocked on Elm's door. "Are you ready to go to Grandpa's?"

"In a minute." He put the map back into his backpack. Opening the door, he said, "Let's see if Randy wants to go with us."

They went next door.

"Randy, we're riding our bikes to town. Do you want to go? It's not far—about four miles," Willow said.

"Sure," Randy said.

As they rode down the driveway, Sequoia trailed behind them.

"I was looking out my window last night, and I saw something weird in the forest. Greenish-blue lights were glowing," Randy said.

"Did they come from a rotten log?" Elm asked.

"I don't know. I only saw the lights."

"It's called foxfire. I've only seen them once. About six months ago." Elm glanced at Willow. "How about you?"

"Uh-huh, six months ago, right before the Millers disappeared," she replied.

"Who are the Millers?" Randy furrowed his eyebrows.

"The family that lived in your house before you moved there," Elm said.

"What?" Randy slammed on his brakes.

Elm and Willow skidded to a stop.

"No, no. Calm down," Willow said. "Everyone thinks they just moved away in the middle of the night." Changing the subject, she said, "It's a mile to the sign that says Welcome to Oak Valley. Let's race." She pumped her legs, leaving Elm and Randy behind.

"Hey, no fair," Randy yelled.

Elm passed Willow on a small incline. She always lost the race at this point. Elm skidded to a stop, then Willow, and Randy last.

They stopped next to the welcome sign.

"Phew!" Randy sucked in shallow breaths. "Next time, I plan to win."

Elm panted. "You can see the whole town from here." As they continued into town, he tried to sound like a tour guide. "Now coming up on your left...the Underwood Family Nursery and Tree Service. We're now turning on to Main Street where the town square is located." Two blocks later, he said, "This is the town's famous Victorian haunted house."

"A haunted house?" Randy stared at the building.

"It's the town's library," Willow said. "It's just a story people tell. I've never seen a ghost, and I go there all the time."

"I can't wait to see inside it," Randy said.

The crack of thunder sounded in the distance.

"Let's hurry before it starts raining," Elm said. "One more block and we'll be at Grandpa's."

They pedaled down First Street just as a downpour started.

"Hurry. See the white cottage with blue shutters? That's Grandpa's."

They rushed onto the porch, carrying their bikes with them.

Willow touched the wind chimes tinkling in the breeze. "Grandpa said the chimes keep evil spirits away." She giggled. "He also said they keep the birds off the porch."

"Hey, Grandpa!" Elm called out.

"What took you so long?" A tall man with white hair and a short beard stood in the doorway. He could pass for Santa Claus except he didn't have a potbelly. "At least you made it here before you got soaked."

25

"We gave Randy a tour around town," Elm said.

"I'm glad you included me." Grandpa laughed. "Nice to meet you, Randy. Are you ready to eat and maybe hear a story?

"What's for lunch?" Willow asked.

"Grilled cheese sandwiches, homemade tomato soup, chips, and cold lemonade." Grandpa led them into the kitchen.

"Yum, I'm starved," Elm said.

"You're always hungry," Willow said.

After they ate, they sat on the sofa in the living room. Sequoia lay next to Grandpa's favorite chair. Grandpa sat down and patted the dog on the head. Leaning forward, he said in a low voice, "Do you believe in magic?"

All three nodded. A clap of thunder rattled the door.

He gulped in some air and whispered, "Monsters."

They scooted closer together on the sofa.

"I've traveled to many places in the world, and I can tell you, there is magic everywhere. Even here in Oak Valley."

"How did magic get here?" Willow asked.

"Centuries ago, a wizard fell in love with a beautiful woman. The woman was afraid of his dark magic. The wizard promised never to use magic again if she would marry him. She agreed. A few days later, she caught him using his magic. She turned her back on him and never spoke to him again."

Randy stared. "The same wizard that lived in the giant house in town?"

"You mean the library?" Grandpa chuckled. "No, I'm not sure a wizard ever lived in the library." Grandpa continued, "The wizard, broken-hearted but furious, placed a curse on her family. Future generations would hear the trees cry when there was trouble, and others in her family would receive magical powers. He also created magical portals around the world. When the portals opened, weird creatures would escape and create havoc."

Elm had heard these stories many times. "Is that a true story? Does it have anything to do with our family?" Elm asked.

Randy tilted his head. "Why would you ask a question like that?"

"Uh, no reason," Elm thought about the tree in the woods. It had actually talked, telling him to come closer.

Grandpa laughed. "No, it's just a story. Do you have magical powers?"

"No." Elm hung his head in embarrassment.

Grandpa sat back, scratched his chin, and began to talk. His baritone voice was hypnotic. "My dad told me this story when I was about your age.

"A long time ago, before the forest became overgrown and people lost their way, a young boy, just a little older than Willow, went into the forest for firewood. He pulled his wagon along behind him. It was a cold, fall evening, and the sun moved toward the horizon. He wanted to be home before complete darkness overtook the woods. The wagon was almost full, but he needed one more limb. He spotted the perfect one, just below an oak tree. When he reached under the large branches, the ground moved. Before he could take a step back, the roots of the tree entangled his legs, climbed up his body, wrapped around his arms, and pulled him underground."

Elm fell forward off the sofa.

"Are you all right?" Grandpa stared at Elm on the floor.

"Yeah, I guess I was sitting to close to the edge. I just kinda slid off."

Randy was so interested in the story he didn't even realize Elm was on the floor. "What happened next?"

"Gee, thanks, I'm fine." Elm bumped Randy as he climbed back on the sofa.

Grandpa said, "Okay, here's what happened."

"Scared and desperate to find his way home, he followed a long, curvy trail. It led through many different territories where he encountered strange and unusual creatures. He had red jasper stones in his pocket, which he gave to several monsters. They helped him find his way."

"What kind of monsters?" Randy asked.

"Not sure. My dad left that to my imagination. The boy eventually found his way home, and he never went into the forest again."

Grandpa stopped talking. He took a drink of water, then cleared his throat. "My dad told me the most important thing to remember is that you should always carry red jasper crystals with you for good luck. So, on that note, I have something to give you." Grandpa went into the other room and came back with three reddish-brown, smooth, shiny stones. "These are jasper stones. Put them in your pockets and keep them with you. They will bring you luck and protection."

"Elm, show Grandpa what's in your backpack," Willow said.

Elm's eyes shot daggers toward Willow. He turned toward his grandpa. "Gee, Grandpa, nothing unusual." He pulled out a whistle, a compass, and a small flashlight. He turned the bag upside down and shook it. Nothing else fell out because he held the map against the inside of the pack with two fingers.

"That reminds me," Grandpa said. "Don't forget, we're going camping in two weeks. Randy, if your parents agree, you can go with us."

"I've never been camping. What do you do?"

"We'll pitch tents, build a campfire, go fishing, hike the hills, play games, and tell stories," Grandpa said.

"Sure! I want to go."

"Looks like you kids are in luck. The sun is shining."

"Thanks for lunch." They shuffled out the door.

Elm smiled. "I told you Grandpa's a great storyteller."

"Does your Dad tell stories like him?" Randy asked.

"No," Willow said. "Grandpa's the only one in the family with the gift of making fables sound like real life. He told us once that Sequoia was over one hundred years old."

"He's very active for seven hundred dog years," Randy said, laughing. "Do you think your grandpa will tell scary stories around the campfire? I can't wait to go. I'm sure I'll sleep with my flashlight on all night."

"I hope not. I don't want to hear scary stories while we're camping," Willow said.

Elm ignored Willow on the ride home. He was annoyed she had tried to get him to show Grandpa his map. He rode next to Randy and listened to him and Willow talk about camping.

Once they were home, Elm said, "See you tomorrow." Then he turned to Willow and whispered, "We're going into the forest tomorrow."

"No, we're not!" she said.

"Yes, we are." He turned and walked into the house.

In his room, he pulled the map out and checked it again. It didn't make any sense. None of the terrain on the map was anywhere near their home or the town. Maybe it was just a map someone had drawn and then tossed away. But the warning to stay out of the forest, and the enormous tree in the center of the map, meant it was definitely their woods. He folded up the map and placed it in his backpack.

Chapter 6

Into the Forest

There was a knock at the door. Before Elm opened it, his mom told him that Randy's parents had called last night asking if Randy could spend a couple of days with them.

Randy stood on the porch with a bag of clothes in his hands. As Elm opened the door, Randy entered, telling Elm, "When Mom told me she and Dad were going to visit my grandparents, I pleaded with them not to take me. I told her that we already made plans, and I didn't want to go. Thanks to your mom, I'm here."

The smell of bacon frying made both their stomachs growl.

"Time for breakfast. I'm starved," Elm said.

They gathered around the table while Mrs. Underwood scooped up fried eggs and bacon and placed it on their plates along with buttermilk biscuits. Elm and Randy grabbed their forks and shoveled eggs into their mouths. Willow glanced at her mom, then ate her eggs slowly.

Sinking his teeth into a strip of crispy bacon Elm chewed, then said, "After breakfast, let's go to the treehouse and make plans."

He then slathered butter on his biscuit, squished some eggs between the two pieces of bread, and shoved half of it into his mouth.

"Willow," he said as crumbs from the biscuit fell from his mouth, "when we're done eating, we'll meet you at the treehouse. I need to get a few things from my room first." He shoved the rest of his biscuit along with the bacon into his mouth and mumbled around it, "C'mon, Randy."

Randy grabbed the last piece of bacon and raced up the stairs behind Elm.

"Did you bring the jasper stone?" Elm asked.

"Yeah, got it in my pocket."

Elm picked up his backpack and scanned the room. He picked up his jasper stone and placed it in his pocket. Into the pack he stuffed three flashlights and one extra-long rope.

"I don't know what you're planning, but do you want this?" Randy held up binoculars.

"Great idea. I don't have any more room in my backpack. Will you carry them?" He grabbed a blue cap off the bed and situated it with the visor just above his eyes.

They charged back down the stairs and out the back door. Once in the treehouse, they found Willow sitting with her backpack.

"What the heck? You brought a pack too. What's in it?" Randy said.

"I just had a weird feeling we might need this later." She dumped her bag. On the floor of the treehouse lay a bag of cookies, six peanut butter and jelly sandwiches, and three bottles of water.

"Did you bring your jasper stone?" Elm asked.

She fished in her pocket and pulled out the shiny stone.

"Both of you are weird." Randy laughed.

Elm was just about to pull the map from his backpack when suddenly Randy jumped up and shouted, "Hey! The lights are glowing in the forest."

Elm grabbed the binoculars and looked. "Let's find the lights!" he said with excitement. It was his plan all along to go into the forest, but the lights now gave him an excuse.

"No, we're not allowed in the forest," Willow said.

"You can stay here. Randy and I are going. Right?" He bumped Randy.

"Is it safe?" Randy asked.

"The lights aren't very far into the trees. I've been there before, and nothing bad has ever happened," Elm said.

34

"Willow, you need to come with us," Randy urged.

She stood with her hands on her hips and a wary look on her face. She shook her head. Elm and Randy climbed down and crossed through the trees in the backyard. Willow grabbed her backpack and scurried down the tree and hurried to catch up with them. Sequoia trailed at a distance.

They stood at the fence posts, looking at each other indecisively. Elm stepped across the boundary line, then Randy and Willow. Their shoes sank into the soft, green moss like walking on a thick carpet.

"Ow!" Randy cried out. He stumbled after getting his foot caught in a tangle of tree roots that crisscrossed the path.

"Are you okay, city boy?" Elm asked.

"Yeah, how much farther?" Randy rubbed his ankle.

"There it is." Elm pointed.

They circled the log, and Randy picked up a small stick. He poked at it, causing the lights to brighten. When he stabbed it a second time, a flurry of fireflies flew up in their faces, making them stumble backward. The fireflies flew into the treetops.

"Ugh! Bugs," Randy said swatting the air in front of him.

"That was amazing," Elm said.

"Okay, let's go back home," Willow said.

"Not yet. Just a little farther," Elm pleaded. "There's something I've been planning to tell you, but since we're here, I'll show you."

Thick undergrowth blocked their view on both sides of the path.

"I don't remember all these branches crisscrossing the path. It will take forever to get to thc clearing," Elm said.

"Are you sure you're going the right direction?" Willow said.

"Yes—" Elm placed his fingers to his lips.

They stood in silence and listened to twigs breaking nearby. Then leaves rustled. Suddenly, a raccoon crossed their path. They stared at each other as they let out the breath, they didn't realize they were holding. Owls asleep in the trees began to screech. Then, abruptly, everything went silent.

Randy said, "Did you hear that?"

"It was an owl," Elm said.

"Not the owl. Someone called my name." He turned. "That way."

"We need to go back home," Willow said as the twigs broke not far from where they were standing.

"We've come this far. Just a little farther," Elm pleaded.

A few more steps and they emerged into a clearing.

"What kind of tree is that?" Randy asked.

"It's a live oak," Elm replied.

"I know it's alive," Randy said.

"That's the name of the tree. It's like the trees you saw in town, except supersized."

A light wind blew, causing whirlwinds to stir the dust. Dirt devils formed and crisscrossed in front of them. The Spanish moss reached out and touched Willow, weaving itself into her hair and pulling her closer.

"Elm!" she screamed. "Help me."

Both boys ran over. Elm held Willow's hair in one hand as he tugged on the moss with the other. It almost sounded like the moss let out a giggle as it released Willow's hair. Elm stared at the moss in his hand, then the wind blew it away from him.

"I want to go home," Willow cried.

Whispers in the air surrounded Elm. He knew it came from the nearby pine trees. The word was repeated over and over.

"Run!"

Elm whirled around. "I agree, let's go home."

Randy yelled, "Help! The roots of the tree! They've wrapped around my ankles. I can't move."

The pines began to chatter. "Don't go under— don't go under..." The cries grew louder.

Willow locked eyes with Elm. "Do you hear the trees?"

Elm raised his eyebrows. "This can't be happening. What should we do?"

"We have to help him."

"One of us needs to get Mom and Dad," he said.

37

"We don't have time."

They moved under the branches of the tree. The wind howled, and the Spanish moss fell around them like a curtain, blocking their view.

The live oak tree's roots slithered around all of them and pulled them underground.

Sequoia jumped into the hole, following the kids. The wind stopped.

Chapter 7

Beneath the Tree

Screaming, they tumbled downward, through the roots of the live oak tree. Elm landed with a thump. Surrounded by darkness, he was unable to see what had crunched beneath him as he hit bottom. But the stench in the air made him gag.

Willow grunted and Randy moaned. Elm reached his trembling hand into his backpack and felt the flashlight. Wrapping his fingers around it, he pulled it from his bag, pushed the button, and there was light.

Randy hung upside down with his foot tangled in the roots. The roots shook, and Randy dropped to the ground. He rolled over into a sitting position and scooted backward.

Elm guided his light toward a grunting noise. Willow lay on the ground, her leg bent at a strange angle beneath her.

"Willow! Your leg! It's broken." Elm heard how shrill his voice sounded.

She rolled onto her side, and her leg popped out from under her. Touching it, she said, "A little sore, but no broken bones. What's that smell?"

Rocking back and forth, Randy whimpered, "No, no, this is not real. I must be dreaming." Looking toward Elm, he said, "Where are we? It's just a dream, right? Where are we? What's happening?"

"Will...Willow! We're...we're under the live oak tree," Elm stuttered.

"No! It's not possible! That's ridiculous. We can't be underground," Willow replied.

"What are you two talking about? I'm having a nightmare. It's time for me to wake up." Randy's voice quivered.

Willow and Randy located their flashlights at the same time. Turning them on, they shined the light toward Elm. Gasping, they covered their noses and mouths with their hands.

"Elm!" Willow sucked in her breath, then coughed from the stench.

"It's only a dream, only a dream," Randy repeated over and over.

Animal bones surrounded Elm. The crunching sound he heard when he landed was from small carcasses. Tangled and swinging from the roots above his head hung decomposing animal bodies. He yelped as he leaped toward the others.

A low rumbling caused all three to turn their flashlights in the direction of Sequoia. The rumble in his throat evolved into a full, ferocious snarl.

"It's only—"

"Shut up and move," Willow muttered then grabbed Randy's arm and scrambled backward. Elm moved with them.

Hundreds of menacing black eyes along the main tree root stared at them. A small hole in the root moved, and a thunderous voice said, "Well, well, well, what do I have here among my roots?"

Moving its many eyes, it said, "Sequoia, my old friend, it's nice to see you again."

Sequoia's growls grew louder.

"Sequoia," Elm whispered. "Is it true you were here with great-grandpa?"

The dog nodded his head.

The roots laughed. "Sequoia is a very old dog. He was enchanted a long time ago to be the guardian of the Underwood family." Its eyes slid toward Willow and Elm. "I'm surprised to see the Underwood children here. I've been watching you for a long time. I remember when your great-grandfather came to visit me. It seems like just the other day."

Elm tried to sound threatening, but he only produced a squeak. "We're going to destroy you when we get back home. You'll never harm any people or animals again."

One of the many roots creaked and groaned, then whipped around his throat, pulling him closer to its mouth. Elm scrunched his eyes closed, sure he was about to be swallowed whole.

Willow and Randy jumped up. "No!" they both screamed. Willow swayed but continued to stand.

Sequoia sprang onto the tangle of roots and bit down. The root released Elm, and red sap spewed from its wound. It roared. "I've heard that threat before from your great-grandfather. You can see I'm still standing, and I will stand for another hundred years."

Willow and Randy took a step back and stumbled to the ground again.

The root turned its attention to Randy. Its eyes widened, and its mouth let out a terrifying laugh. "I'm surprised to see you, boy. I never thought I would catch a wolf in my roots."

"How...how do you know my name?" Randy stuttered.

Another blood-curdling laugh. "Not your name, boy. It's your blood. The scent of a wolf is all over you."

Elm and Willow glanced at Randy out of the corner of their eyes.

"I...I don't know what it's talking about. I don't have wolf blood. Don't look at me like that." Randy seemed confused. Sequoia wagged his tail and nuzzled up to Randy. "See, Sequoia knows I'm not a wolf."

"What parents don't tell their children. You, boy, yes, you have wolf blood in your veins. You'll understand soon when you turn twelve. Wolves have keen hearing. That's how you heard me call your name when no one else did. And you two, why didn't you listen to the trees? Didn't they tell you not to go under my branches? Why would you cross into an area you've been forbidden to enter?"

"Listen to the trees?" Elm asked.

"You've heard the trees talk your whole life. Maybe not with your ears, but that nagging sixth sense when there was danger in the woods. Now you're older. You can hear the trees. You can even talk to them, and they will answer, maybe."

"How?" Willow asked.

"I'm sure you heard the story of a wizard and his fiancé. Did your parents not tell you the fiancé was your ancient grandmother? Your family is cursed."

"Grandpa's stories," Elm whispered to Willow.

As the root continued to ramble on, they moved farther away.

The tree root creaked and yawned. "I'm tired. I haven't had so many visitors tangled in my roots in a long time. Be on your way, but know this—my roots spread far and wide. I'll be watching you." The eyes closed, and the root went silent.

They took a few steps, and the root opened its eyes again, yawning. "Be careful. You never know what you'll run into underground." The tree let out a menacing laugh. They turned and ran.

Chapter 8

A New World

Sprinting down the trail in darkness with only the flashlights to guide them, Elm felt uneasy. He continued to glance over his shoulder, thinking the roots could sliver toward them to drag them back at any moment. He wondered if they would ever see daylight or home again.

Randy, just in front of Elm, said, "It's getting brighter. The sun must be coming up."

"What sun? We're underground," Willow said.

"Sun, moon, or artificial light—at least we can see," Elm said. "I think we should look at this adventure as our camping trip. We'll sleep outside and explore new surroundings." He tried to make their unfortunate circumstances sound exciting. He didn't want the others to know how frightened he was, and after all, it was his fault they were underground.

No longer in the dark, Elm knelt on one knee, removed his cap, and pulled the map from his backpack. Randy bent over his shoulder and watched him unfold the map and lay it on the ground. The brittle edges crumbled and dissolved into the dirt.

"What the heck is that? You knew! You knew all along that this would happen if we went under that tree." Randy paced back and forth.

"No, I didn't. I didn't even know the tree existed until a few days ago. That's the same time I found this map," Elm replied.

"Sure." Randy scoffed. "Why didn't you tell me about it then?"

"It was never the right time. Someone was always around. My parents or your parents. I'm showing it to you now." Elm lowered his eyes. He knew he had kept the map a secret.

Sequoia growled.

"Okay, guys, you're upsetting the dog." Willow scratched Sequoia's ears. "We're here, and we need to find our way home. We have very few supplies or food. I know Elm just recently found the map. He showed it to me. I didn't really pay much attention to it. I thought it was part of a game. Maybe it will help us find our way and get us out of this nightmare."

They sat next to each other and stared at the map. Elm wondered how long it would take them to find their way home.

"Are you kidding me?" Randy gasped. "Look at all the warnings."

Elm reread the map. "If this is truly a map of the underground, then we must be headed to Razor Mountain. The only thing we have to remember is to stay on the path. That sounds easy enough."

"Then to the Land of Fire where there are wild horses," Willow said. "That doesn't sound safe. We will either get burned or trampled to death."

"Let's just worry about one area at a time." Elm folded the map and put it back into his pack. He wiped sweat from his brow, then pulled the bill of his cap down over his forehead. "Are you ready to go?"

They gathered their packs and continued down the path.

Randy took a deep breath, then asked, "Can you honestly hear the trees talk?"

Elm shrugged, then answered, "It's just been a feeling. I've never heard the trees say words until today when they told us not to go under the oak. What about you?" Elm glanced at Willow.

It was then he noticed as she walked, she placed her weight more on one leg than the other as she walked. "How is your leg?"

"It hurts, but I'll make it," she said with a slight grimace as she took a step. "You know, I heard the

47

trees tell us to run out of the water, one time when we were at the lake. I also heard them again today."

"Hmm." Elm turned to Randy. "Now, why did the tree roots say you had wolf blood?"

"I have no idea what it was talking about. Ugh!" Randy cried out as he jumped and flung his arms around.

"Ew, get it out of my hair," Willow cried, walking backward and rubbing her face. "I feel bugs crawling all over me."

Elm's shirt moved against his skin. He jerked it over his head and threw it down. He then stood behind Willow, checking her hair and clothes. "There's nothing there." He stooped down, picked up his shirt, and not seeing any creatures, put it back on.

Sequoia sat off to the side, licking his fur.

"That felt creepy. It was like walking through a million spider webs," Randy said.

They glanced back—no webs covered the pathway.

Moving at a snail's pace, they checked out their new surroundings. Off to one side stood a grove of pine and elm trees. On the other side—bushes and flowers.

"These flowers make me think of home." Willow sighed.

Coming to the top of a small incline on the path, Elm paused and pointed across the field. "This must be Razor Mountain."

"Holy smokes." Randy's jaw dropped. "Let's check it out."

"No!" Willow grabbed Randy's arm. "It looks dangerous. And the map said to stay on the path."

"I thought this was supposed to be an adventure. We need to explore," Randy grumbled.

Past an open meadow filled with tall, wild grasses and next to a grove of trees stood a majestic range of jagged and razor-sharp stone formations. The saw-toothed peaks rose high into the skyline, ripping floating clouds apart. The glare of the sun made the tips look like they were covered with dark red, dried blood.

Sequoia sniffed the air and whimpered.

"What's wrong, boy?" Elm glanced in the direction Sequoia was staring.

The grass swayed in the breezeless air.

"There's something in the grass and it's coming this way," Elm whispered.

"What do you think it is?" Willow asked.

"I don't know. Stay on the path and keep moving."

"I agree," Randy nodded. "The oak tree said your family was cursed by the wizard. Besides hearing trees talk, do either of you have magic?"

"No," they answered in unison.

Terry Nolan

"Too bad. We could probably use some," Randy said.

They moved slowly until a head popped above the grass. Willow gasped as several more surfaced. Grabbing each other's hands, they rushed down the path. They stopped suddenly when the grass parted and a pack of short humanoids blocked their way. Large round red eyes bulged from the humanoids' sockets. Short noses turned upward like a pig's snout. Worst of all they had long fingernails, sharp and piercing. Dozens of the hobbit-like people moved onto the path.

"Let's not frighten them. Maybe they're friendly." Randy took a step back.

The lead humanoid squealed like a pig. Sequoia let out a howl and raced toward them. The front row of beings raised its arms and slashed the dog with their razor-sharp nails. He yelped and fell to his side. The creatures surrounded him, licking their lips.

"No! Sequoia!" Willow screamed.

"Hurry! We have to save him," Elm cried. "Watch out for their hands. Kick the little monsters back into the grass."

They raced toward the attacking humanoids.

"Take that!" Willow swung her backpack, knocking several monsters off the path.

Elm whacked one with his rucksack, making it fly into the air. It landed hundreds of yards away.

50

While Willow and Elm fought the humanoids with their backpacks, Randy fell to his knees and scooped up the eighty-pound dog. He carried him to a safe area on the path.

"The path is clear," Randy yelled.

Elm and Willow rushed to Sequoia. He thumped his tail against the path, then licked his side. They knelt, and Elm moved the fur and found only a few nicks. Sequoia rubbed against Randy's hand.

"You're welcome, boy." Randy scratched the top of the dog's head.

"Thanks, man. How did you lift him?" Elm asked.

"I don't know. I guess adrenalin kicked in," Randy replied.

Elm squeezed his eyes shut for a moment. What other dangers lay ahead? Would they ever make their way back home?

"Holy crap!" Randy yelled.

Elm opened his eyes. On the path behind them, the creatures crawled on their hands and knees, causing Elm to think of lizards chasing prey. The humanoids lifted their heads, letting out primal screams that caused their whole body to shake. Elm bolted upright and yelled, "Run!"

They ran for their lives. Unexpectedly, Sequoia, Willow, and Randy disappeared. Elm turned and saw the humanoids only feet away. He didn't know what had happened to the others, but he stayed on the path, then he felt a web-like substance.

"Yuck!" Randy said.

"I think we slid through another invisible wall. Look," Elm said.

They watched the humanoids search for them. The hobbit people were not able to move through or see the wall. Making loud grunting noises, the creatures walked back into the tall grass.

"What were those things?" Randy gasped for air.

A wicked cackle vibrated from a nearby tree. They whirled around and saw two black holes in the tree staring at them. A third hole below the others, moved, and the tree spoke.

"Hobbits are from the stone mountains. You made it through your first trial. Now, we'll see if you can make it through the next one." The tree roared with laughter, then the holes in the tree vanished.

Chapter 9

First Night

The pounding of Elm's heart slowed as they left the invisible wall behind and moved up a slight grade leading to a wider path. They sat down to rest after their harrowing experience. Elm turned his cap around backward, then pulled the map from his backpack.

"Is everyone okay?" Elm said.

Willow lowered her head and sighed.

"What?" Elm asked.

"First, I've been stabbed by monster humanoids, and my legs hurt. Second, we've traveled through an invisible wall. Where are we?" Willow bent over and rubbed her legs.

"I thought hobbits were meek and mild—nice, tiny people. At least that's how they seem in the books I read," Randy said. "I have a few stabs too. Did your grandpa mention any of this in his stories?" He raised his eyebrows, wrinkling his forehead.

"No," Elm muttered.

"Are we in the Land of Fire?" Willow checked the map.

"I don't think we're there yet," Elm said.

"We have to go through fire then into the Fairy Kingdom. I wonder if the fairies are as mean as the hobbits?" Randy touched the map. Several pieces crumbed and dissolved into the dirt.

"Hey, be careful," Elm said.

"I wish we had paper and a pencil. We could draw the map before it falls apart," Willow said.

"If we stay on the path, we'll find our way," Elm said.

"Sure, depending on what's chasing us," Randy said.

Elm folded the map carefully and placed it back in his pack. They continued their journey. Sequoia led the way. The new area had more tree roots crisscrossing the path. Elm sensed a presence watching them. It all seemed very peaceful. A little too peaceful.

They had walked for a couple of hours when the path led them into a tunnel.

"Hey, look," Randy pointed to a large, round shaft opened above him. He yelled, "Anybody up there? Help! We're down here."

"Stop yelling," Willow snapped. "No one will hear you. We're under an abandoned well. It seems we've been walking a long distance, yet we haven't traveled very far from home."

"What do you mean?" Randy asked.

"This well isn't far from our house," Elm said. "I have an idea. If we crawl on each other's shoulders, do you think we can reach the top?"

Randy nodded.

"We can try." Willow shrugged her shoulders.

Sequoia whined and licked Elm's hand. "Not now, boy. We're almost home."

The dog whimpered, sat down, and watched.

"I'll be the base," Elm said. "I'm sure I can hold both of you." Elm dropped to his hands and knees.

Randy stepped on Elm's back. "Ow! Be careful. Try to put one foot around my shoulders and the other on my butt."

Randy started over. Holding Willow's hand, he stepped up. Elm took a deep breath as he supported Randy's weight on his back. Randy swayed right, then left. He placed his fingertips against the walls and steadied himself. Elm's arms began to quivered from the strain.

Willow put one foot near Elm's butt, then jumped up and grabbed Randy's waist. He let out a giggle. She pulled herself up and reached for Randy's shoulders.

Elm didn't realize he was holding his breath until he let out a "humph." His arms shook, and his elbows bent from all the weight. He fell flat on his stomach. Randy and Willow tumbled off. The light above flickered as dust curled up the shaft.

"Sorry, I can't hold both of you." Elm panted and his stomach grumbled. "Did you hurt yourself when you fell?"

Randy laughed. "No, Willow tickled me, and I couldn't hold on to the wall."

"I'm not hurt, but I'm hungry. Let's eat while we have light to see by." Willow pulled the water bottles out of her pack. "I have peanut butter and jelly sandwiches, and a bag of cookies." She held out two halves of a sandwich along with two cookies, and Elm and Randy accepted it. "We'll need to ration our food."

She gave a cookie to Sequoia. He gobbled it up and sat waiting for more.

At first, they laughed about their attempt to climb up the well. They hadn't really had a chance to enjoy anything since being dragged underground. Then Elm changed the mood.

"So, you have wolf blood in you," Elm mumbled with peanut butter in his mouth. He took a sip of water. "No wonder you had the strength to lift Sequoia."

Randy clenched his hand into a fist. "I don't have wolf blood. I am not a werewolf or any other type of wolf. Your family is the one with all the weird stories about underground travels and guess what, here we are. And you can hear trees talk."

"Don't talk about my grandpa. I didn't know about the tree." Elm stood up and stared down at Randy. Randy jumped up and stood face-to-face with him.

"Stop it! Stop quibbling. Oh my gosh! I sound like Mom." Willow wrapped her arms around herself and glared at Elm. "We have to work together to find our way out of this mess. Let's hope Grandpa's story will help us. Randy, if you are part wolf, it could come in handy."

"I'm not!" Randy snapped. "So what if I hear noises better than other people? And happen to be very sensitive to smells? That doesn't mean I'm part wolf. That's crazy. No way."

Elm and Willow didn't respond. They were silent for a while as they sat on the dirt, each in their own dark thoughts and fears of what might lie ahead.

"Ready to continue?" Willow asked.

Elm's eyes shifted to the shaft. He wished they had been able to climb out of this nightmare.

Sequoia took the lead, and everyone fell in line behind him. The tunnel ended, and the path turned dry and dusty. Cracks crossed the ground like wrinkles on an old woman. The toes of Elm's shoes got caught every once in a while, causing him to stumble. Finally, the ground turned soft. Moss covered the path, making walking easier. The light above began to fade.

After hours of hiking, Elm said, "We need to find a safe place to rest before it gets dark."

"How are we supposed to know it's safe?" Randy looked around.

"How do I know?" Elm replied, avoiding eye contact. "Once we find it, we'll have to take turns being on guard."

The path wound through acres of open land. Patches of fruit trees grew on both sides of the trail. Beyond the orchard, the route came to a circle of pines with a few apple trees.

Elm glanced through the trees. "Maybe we can sleep up in the branches."

"I thought you said we couldn't trust the trees. What if they're controlled by the live oak?" Randy asked.

Elm shrugged his shoulders. He didn't have any answers.

As they neared the trees, the largest one said, "Come, children. Come to the grove."

"Did you hear that?" Elm asked.

"I heard it. It was creepy. I don't think we should trust them." Randy shook his head.

"What other choice do we have?" Willow said. "Let's ask them."

The dog moved closer to the trees, wagging his tail.

"Sequoia seems to approve." Elm moved closer to the trees. "Can you help us? May we sleep in your branches tonight?"

"No need to climb. You can sleep on the ground. We will move together to protect you from the herd." The tree's voice sounded like a woman.

"A herd of what?" Randy asked.

"Animals, of course," the tree replied.

"What do you think?" Elm glanced at Willow.

"I'm tired, and I want to rest. I say we trust the trees," Willow replied.

They moved under a tangle of branches and sat down on a fallen log. The trees closed together into a tight circle formation.

"It's a trap!" Elm yelled.

"No," replied the tree. "When you're ready to leave, we'll open the wall for you."

"Where are we?" Elm asked, his voice barely above a whisper.

The tree sounded stunned. "You don't know? How can you travel and not know where you are? You're in the Land of Fire."

"But we haven't seen any fires," Willow said.

"You will. You should rest before the animals arrive. They can smell strangers, you know."

"What animals? I thought you said we were safe here," Randy said.

"You are safe as long as you stay quiet and don't make any noise."

They huddled closer together. They removed their backpacks, and Willow took peanut butter and jelly sandwiches out of her pack and split one between Elm and Randy. She took a half for herself and put the rest back in her pack. She gave each a cookie and one to Sequoia.

"Is this all we get? I'm starving," Randy said.

"We have to conserve our food. We don't have much, and we don't know how long it will take us to get home," Willow said.

No sooner had they finished their meal than the ground shook and the tree branches swayed above. They heard the sound of a neigh, a whinny, and a squeal. They shot up and formed a circle, placing their shoulders together and facing away from each other.

"Do you see anything?" Elm asked.

"No," both Willow and Randy replied.

No way can these trees protect us from whatever's coming. Why had he been so determined to travel into the forbidden forest? And why had he put his sister and friend in harm's way?

A glint of light glowed at a distance. Something large was headed their way. When a flame flared up, Elm narrowed his eyes and stared. *It can't be.*

The roar grew louder along with the thunderous sound of hooves pounding the ground. Sequoia's ears lay back. He let out a long, slow growl.

Randy covered his ears to block the sound of hooves, and Willow put her hand over her mouth and held her breath.

A large, muscular animal stomped past their hiding place. Two long, spiral horns extended from their heads. Fire flowed from their hooves, and they blew smoke from their nostrils.

"Oh my gosh! Horses from hell." The color drained from Elm's face.

The herd circled the outside of the trees. Their hooves pawed the ground as they tromped around. Dust billowed up into the air. The lead horse angled its head so that its gleaming, demonic, red eyes locked onto Elm's. He felt like he was looking into the eyes of the devil. The horse-like creatures snorted, and smoke filled the inside circle of the trees. The other horses lowered their heads and lurched forward, ramming the tree trunks with their horns. The trees trembled, and the ground quaked. With rattled nerves and pounding heart, Elm glanced at Willow.

"How long will the trees withstand this barrage?" Willow asked between coughs.

"We're going to die!" Randy blurted out.

The horses circled the grove. They flared their nostrils as they turned their hindquarters to the trees and bucked them with their flaming hooves. A few blazes shot through the openings and flew past Randy.

The sound of splintering wood caused the three to freeze. A tree dropped three long, thin branches with sharp ends, then said, "Use these as weapons."

"Hurry! Grab a branch." Elm picked one up and stabbed at the horses through the trees.

Willow and Randy grasped the other limbs and went to different areas of the circle. They thrust the branches at the horses.

Before Elm could stop him, Sequoia squeezed through a gap in the trees. He charged the lead horse and bit it on the leg. The leader reared up as Sequoia took off running toward a row of hedges.

Elm shrieked, "No, Sequoia, come back."

The horse chased the dog, stopping when an earsplitting screech was heard in the distance. The other horses lifted their heads and watched the leader. He bucked the bushes where Sequoia hid and set them ablaze, then galloped in the direction of the sound. The other horses dashed after him.

Elm watched the flames blaze, catching nearby bushes on fire. Smoke filled the air. He called out to Sequoia.

Sequoia raced out of the bushes just as several massive pelicans flew over, dropping water and putting out the fire. The birds then flew out of sight.

Sequoia returned to Elm. The dog's fur smelled of smoke and burned hair. Concerned, Elm kneeled and checked the dog's paws. He parted the fur and found a singed area but no serious injuries.

"I think it's time to start moving before they decide to come back," Randy mumbled.

"You're safe now. They won't return. You need to rest. You still have a long journey ahead of you," the calming female voice of the tree said.

"How do you know they won't return? And where did those birds come from?" Elm asked.

"The screech came from a different herd. The horses will fight each other over their territory. The pelicans live near a river. They show up with their throat pouches filled with water whenever they spot a fire or smoke. That is why there is still life in this land of fire. The birds keep the fires under control."

"Amazing" was the only word Elm could think of to say.

Darkness now surrounded them. A cool wind blew through the trees. Elm shivered, not sure if it was from the breeze or the trauma they had endured.

They lay down, and the trees shook their branches. Pine needles fell over the children, covering them like a blanket. They dozed off while Sequoia kept watch.

Chapter 10

Fight or Flight

The following morning, Elm woke to the sun peeking through the trees and hitting him in his eyes. As he squinted, he thought he saw a tree branch reaching for him. Frightened, he jumped up. Looking around, he realized he was safe and they had slept beneath the trees.

Yawning, Randy said, "What a dream." Opening his eyes, he added, "Oh crap, it wasn't a dream."

A voice came from an apple tree. "Good morning. Would you like to have an apple for breakfast?"

Elm and Randy glanced at each other.

Willow quickly replied. "Yes, and if you have any extras that we can take with us, that would be nice."

The tree shook and dropped several apples.

They ate half a sandwich along with an apple, juice running down their chins. Elm sucked on his apple, feeling the juice run down his throat. Even Sequoia gnawed on an apple. Willow picked up the rest of the apples and placed them in her pack.

As the trees parted, one of them said, "Don't forget your spears. You might need them in the future."

Elm hesitated before leaving. He turned around and thanked the trees for their help. Stepping onto the trail, he observed the scorched ground on both sides.

"Phew!" Randy sighed as he looked at the burnt bushes. "Yesterday was a close call. I thought we were going to die."

"That's a terrible thought." Willow touched Elm's arm. "Do you think we'll be safe this morning?"

"Don't worry. As long as we stick together, we'll be fine," Elm said without much conviction. He smiled and put an arm around Willow. "We'll be okay."

They followed a winding path that rose sharply, then declined. Tree roots crisscrossed back and forth, making walking a chore.

Randy stumbled, falling face first to the ground. "I swear that root tripped me on purpose. Do you think it's part of the oak tree?"

"No way. We've traveled too far. Tree roots usually don't spread any farther than the tree is tall," Elm said.

"Sure, but that's with nonmagical trees," Willow said.

"Well, I still don't think" Elm tripped on a root. His hands flew out in front of him to soften his fall, but he scraped against a sharp knob on the root, slicing his skin. He let out a yelp as he rolled over, grabbing the injured area with his other hand.

Eye to eye with a thick root, he peered into a hole.

It whispered, "I'm watching you. You're not going to make it back home."

Elm jumped up and cried out.

"Elm, your hand," Willow cried.

"The root talked to me," Elm slung his hand, a trickle of blood flying into the air.

"What did it say?" Randy said.

"It's watching us." He didn't mention the rest of the conversation.

"I hear the pounding of horse hooves," Randy yelled. "Let's get out of here."

Elm felt the vibration before he heard the sound of the hooves. He whirled around with his weapon in his hand. Prickles of sweat formed across his forehead. He stood motionless in terror. He could now see the horses with their feet ablaze in the distance. The hairs on the back of his neck stood up.

"Run!" Willow shouted.

"We can't outrun horses, and I don't see anywhere to hide. We must fight." Elm's weapon slipped from his perspiring hands. He quickly retrieved it.

Willow and Randy grabbed their weapons and ran to Elm's side. They stood side by side while Sequoia moved in front of them.

"I don't know how to fight." Randy's voice trembled with dread. "I don't want to die."

Elm felt like he was in a dream as he watched the lead horse gallop closer. Randy thrust his weapon but missed. Smoked billowed from the horse's nostrils. Sequoia rushed under the horse's belly and bit into its stomach. The horse rocked back on its hind legs, blood gushing from the wound. A low-pitched, guttural sound came from its mouth.

Willow moved to the side and stabbed it in its hindquarters. The horse kicked her in the stomach, knocking the breath out of her. She fell to the ground, pulling her legs toward her chest and holding her stomach.

Elm finally shook the fog from his mind. He saw Randy run toward the horse, but the animal turned its back to him and faced Elm.

The horse studied Elm for a moment, then stretched its neck and chomped down on Elm's backpack. It swung its head high in the air and let go of the pack. Screaming, Elm sailed across an open field, his arms flailing in the air. He felt himself dropping before he crashed on the ground in a sandpit. He groaned in agony.

Elm was just lifting his head when Willow and Randy leaped into the pit beside him. Sequoia had been lying beside him.

"Elm!" Willow cried. "Are you all right?"

A wave of queasiness shook him. He glanced at a large boulder only inches from his head. If he had landed on it, he would be dead. He raised up and gave a weak smile. "I'm okay."

Together they crawled to the top of the pit. Peering over the edge, they watched the horses. The lead horse let out a squeal and pawed the ground. The pack replied with snorts. They all turned and trotted in the opposite direction.

"They're leaving," Elm said.

Willow carried Elm's backpack while Randy helped Elm out of the pit. He placed Elm's arm over his shoulder and around his neck. Elm leaned against him as they moved back to the path.

"Do you need to rest?" Randy said.

"No. Let's keep going." Elm hobbled along without being helped.

They resumed their journey. An hour later, they passed through another invisible wall.

Chapter 11

Fairy Help

Elm's eyelids fluttered. His body hunched over, and he swayed back and forth. He felt light-headed, then his feet tangled together, and he landed on the ground.

His throat parched, he whispered, "Do you have any water?" *Do I have a concussion?*

Willow and Randy shared a concerned look. Willow quickly retrieved a bottle of water from her pack and handed it to Elm.

"Drink slowly," she said.

"I'm surprised you made it this far," Randy said. "You are one lucky guy. When I saw you flying across the field, I was sure you would end up with broken bones. Sorry about your cap. It flew in a different direction."

After drinking some water, Elm felt better. He reached up and touched the top of his head. "I didn't even know it was missing. Will you look in my backpack? I have another one."

"You're kidding," Randy said as he pulled out a black baseball cap with a white hawk on it.

Willow giggled. "He always has a spare cap in his bag."

"What is it with you and caps?" Randy handed the cap to him.

"I don't know. I think when I was really young, my hair was light and thin. My mom told me I looked bald. That's when I started wearing caps. Now my hair is thick and dark, but hats make me feel calm."

"You definitely need to feel calm here." Randy stood up and surveyed their surroundings. "Hey, we're back home. This is the forest behind your house."

"Finally." Willow clapped her hands together.

Elm looked up, trying to get his bearings, then shook his head. "Sorry, guys, we're not home. We're sitting where the fence posts should be. Look behind us—there are no trees, no treehouse, and no house. We just have a path in front of us."

"Well, at least it seems familiar. It makes me feel better." Willow smiled.

"Let's check out the map," Elm said.

"We're in Fairy Kingdom. It doesn't look very big. Maybe we can cross it in a day," Willow said.

"I hope it's a friendly kingdom. Troll Territory is next, and I've never heard of a friendly troll," Randy said.

Elm put the map away, and this time it didn't crumble. They entered the kingdom and stepped over gnarled roots of massive trees. They traveled for hours over terrain that led them up a slope. When they reached the crest of a hill, Randy pointed to a rotten log.

"There's a fairy fire." He picked up a stick and poked the moss-covered stump. Hundreds of fireflies flew into the air and lit up the area up like an explosion from a Roman candle.

A firefly landed on Willow's hand. Her eyes widened as she moved her hand closer to her face. "Oh my." It wasn't a firefly. A tiny lady with wings appeared. "It's a fairy."

"What?" Randy stared at his arm as his eyes bulged. Looking around, he said, "They're everywhere."

Once a fairy touched their skin, they could see all the fireflies were fairies.

"No way," Elm said.

"Hold out your hand, and let one land on you," Willow said.

Elm turned his palm upward. A firefly stood on his hand and changed into a tiny woman. She had skin that glittered and long flowing hair. Her colorful, translucent wings twinkled with different hues of blue.

The fairies flew all around but avoided Sequoia.

"I guess we're in Fairy Kingdom," Randy said.

Elm and Willow watched as the fairies swarmed around Randy's face. He put his hands up to protect himself but not harm the fairies.

"Hey, what's going on?" Randy cried out.

The fairies yelled in unison. "Do you see any males around here? This is not Fairy Kingdom—it's the Fairy Queendom."

Elm and Willow laughed.

"I'm sorry. I'm so sorry," Randy said. "It's just that the map called it a kingdom."

"How do you survive if there are no males?" Elm said.

The fairies flexed their wings and spun around in a frenzy. One pulled a tiny sword from her waist and stuck it up Elm's nose. "Do you think we can't protect ourselves?"

"Ouch! No. I mean, yes, you can protect yourself, but have there never been any men fairies?" Elm said.

Elm glanced at Willow. She stood a short distance away with a smile on her face as she watched the fairies attack Elm and Randy. He mouthed the words, "Help us."

The fairies flew away from Elm and Randy and formed two lines. At the entrance of the line flew a fairy with a crown on her head. Her bronze skin was flawless. Long, black hair with gray streaks flowed down her back. Her translucent, silver wings sparkled. As she passed the fairies, they curtsied.

Willow had moved next to Elm and Randy. When the fairy stopped in front of them, Willow bumped Elm in the side as she bowed. Elm glanced at Randy, and they both kneeled on one knee.

"Please stand." Her voice was soft and lyrical. "I am Marcelina, the Fairy Queen. To answer your question about the male fairies, they were kidnapped many years ago by the trolls."

"Why?" Elm asked.

"The trolls thought they could take over our land and expand their territory. But so far, they have not succeeded." Marcelina fluttered closer to Elm. "Humans seldom come to this area."

"Can you help us find our way?" Elm asked.

"We can take you only so far."

"Lead the way, beautiful lady," Randy said.

All the fairies giggled. They swarmed above the kids' heads, then started down a trail. "Follow us," one of them said.

"Can we trust them?" Willow exchanged a look with Elm.

"Let's see where they take us," he replied.

They remained alert as they followed the fireflies—fairies—through thorny, overgrown bushes. The spikes poked and scratched them as they squeezed down a narrow pathway. After two hours, they walked through a thicket of trees to a clearing.

Before them swayed a primitive bridge over a raging river. It was held up by thick vines that were anchored by huge boulders. The deck was made from narrow tree branches that hung loosely, ready to fall into the river below. It looked like it would collapse at any minute.

"This is as far as we go," Marcelina said. "We never cross the troll bridge."

"What? Are there trolls under the bridge?" Elm asked.

"No, but other creatures live in the water."

A large fish jumped into the air. No, not a fish— a creature with the head and arms of a monkey and fins and tail of fish. It grinned, showing enormous, crooked teeth.

"Don't go into the water," a fairy with iridescent, red wings said. "These creatures will eat anything that falls into the creek."

A fairy with green-and-yellow striped wings added, "Be very careful while crossing the bridge. When you get to the other side, you will be in Troll Territory. They don't take kindly to strangers roaming their lands. Remember, stay on the path."

"I think we should camp here before we cross into the badlands," Elm said. "I'm tired and still sore from the horse throwing me."

"Badlands. That's funny." Randy chuckled. "As far as I can tell, we've been in the badlands ever since we were pulled underground."

"You should be safe here," Marcelina said.

"Can we drink the water?" Elm asked.

"Yes, but remember, the monkey fish are quick and can drag you into the river if they get a hold on you." The fairies gathered, swarmed into the sky, then disappeared.

"Randy and I will try to fill the water bottles if you will find a place we can rest," Elm said to Willow.

"Don't let one of those little monsters get either one of you," Willow said.

They moved to the edge of the water and peered into the darkness.

"Are you sure this water is drinkable?" Randy asked.

"I only know what the fairies said. I'm so thirsty I have to trust them."

They bent down with their empty water bottles. Ice cold water flowed over Elm's hands. He took a second and swallowed water from the bottle.

"This is delicious. It's cold, and my dry throat feels better," Elm said.

He continued to fill the bottle when, in the distance, he saw a monkey head pop up out of the water, then another, and another. The monkey fish swam toward them.

"Hurry!" Elm urged.

"We could stab it and cook it," Randy said.

Elm chuckled. "Ugh, are you that hungry? City boy, do you know how to skin a monkey or gut a fish?"

"I'm starving, but guess I'll stick to peanut butter and jelly. Let's go."

They found Willow near two trees. She pulled out three halves of peanut butter and jelly sandwich and apples. She handed half to each. "Let's hope we find food in the badlands."

They ate their sandwiches. Elm's stomach growled as he lay down. The feeling from before returned—he felt someone watching him. He glanced toward the river to ensure no monkey fish had crawled out of the water. He glanced around at the trees. What he didn't see was a tree nearby open an eye. Sequoia curled up next to him. The dog's heat warmed him and calmed his nerves. Elm and the others fell asleep.

Chapter 12

Badlands

The next morning, the sun rose over the horizon, filling the sky with a mix of oranges, reds, and blues.

They gathered their belongings and stood at the entrance of the bridge. Elm pulled on the vines that held the bridge up. He took a couple of steps onto the bridge, then backed up.

"It seems sturdy enough," he said.

"It doesn't look very safe," Randy said as the monkey fish leaped in the air inches from the bridge.

Sequoia barked and darted across the bridge.

Elm touched Willow's arm. "Are you ready to cross?"

"Yes." She bit her lip and stepped onto the bridge.

Elm watched her hold the vine rail as her knuckles turned white. A thick, dark-gray mist rose from the water and engulfed the bridge, creating a blinding curtain. He couldn't see her. He shouted, "Willow!" There was no reply.

Several minutes later, Willow called from across the bridge, "I made it."

"You go next," Elm said to Randy.

Randy took his first step. The fog dissipated, but now the cross branches were wet and slippery. Halfway across the bridge, Randy tumbled flat onto the bridge. Elm sucked in his breath. Randy wrapped his hand around the rail and heaved himself up. Finally, Randy made it to the other side and collapsed on the ground.

Elm walked onto the first limb. The bridge creaked and bounced as it swayed back and forth. His stomach tossed as his heart thumped in his ears. A monkey fish jumped and touched his leg, then fell back into the river, splashing water onto the bridge. Elm shivered as he stretched to move from one wet tree branch to another. He didn't even realize he had made it across the bridge until Willow hugged him. With a rush of relief, he took a deep breath.

They huddled together until their nerves calmed down. Standing, they searched their surroundings. Rocks and boulders covered the barren land.

"We've been walking for days. We can't still be under Oak Valley," Randy complained. "Are we ever going to find our way above ground?"

"All I know is we have to follow the path." Elm pulled the map out of his pack. He slowly unfolded it. "This is where we are, Troll Territory, and I think this is the path home." He folded the map in half—it disintegrated.

Elm's eyes widened, and he scraped the ground with his hands, but it was no use. The map was gone.

"No! What did you do? How are we going to find our way? I want to go home." Willow's voice rose with anxiety as tears streamed down her face.

"I'm sorry! I didn't do it. It just fell apart." Elm stared at the ground. *Again, I let everyone down. Everything that goes wrong is my fault.*

"This is just great. What are we going to do now?" Randy ran his hand through his hair.

Elm snatched his backpack and stood up. "I didn't do it." He kicked the dirt, then took his cap off and slapped it against his leg. He put the baseball cap back on and started walking. *Maybe Willow and Randy would be better off without me.*

"Elm, stop," Willow cried. "You can't leave us. We need you."

Elm waited for them to catch up. They walked in silence. Morning turned to afternoon, and the landscape returned to trees and rolling hills. The moon would be up in a few hours.

"I smell food." Randy's stomach growled.

"I see smoke rising. Looks like it's just over the next hill," Elm said.

79

Sequoia led the way. He ventured off the path toward the scent of roasting meat.

"Wait," Willow begged. "We can't leave the path. The fairies said we'd get lost."

"You can stay. I'm starving, and I'm not going to pass up food," Randy replied.

Mumbling all the way, Willow followed the boys. When Sequoia reached the crest of the hill, he lay down. Elm glanced at Randy and made a downward hand motion. They crawled the short distance and joined Sequoia. Willow brought up the rear.

Randy looked through the binoculars. "I think we've found the trolls' village."

Willow snatched the binoculars. She clamped her hand over her mouth then whispered to Elm. "Are they human?"

"Trolls," Elm whispered.

Gathered around a kettle on a campfire stood a group of enormous humans with long, straggly hair. They wore helmets with horns protruding from each side. Jagged teeth overhung from their large mouths, and tusks jutted from their lower lips. They had enormous hands with clawed nails and wore heavy animal pelts even though the weather was quite warm. They seemed to be laughing and pointing at the stew or whatever was in the kettle.

"Oh no." Willow handed the binoculars to Elm. "Look in the trees."

Different size cages swung from tree branches. Three held humans. From a distance, it looked like a man in one, a woman in another, and a child in the third. The cages hung from large hooks drilled into the limbs. Other cages held giant rabbits, a baby wolf, and eagles. Instead of hanging on hooks, the trolls had thrown ropes over the branch and then tied the ropes to the trunk of the tree.

"Oh my gosh, we have to get out of here. Let's get back to the path," Willow said.

Elm stared open mouthed at her. "Are you serious? We can't leave people hanging in cages. What if it were us up there? Wouldn't you want someone to save you?"

"But how? We're just kids," Willow said.

"We'll go back down the hill and make a plan."

Randy didn't argue with either of them. They moved noiselessly.

"Ah woooo!"

Randy jumped. "That doesn't sound good. What is it?"

"Sounds like a wolf," Elm said.

"Trolls. Wolves. We can't fight both of them." Willow glanced in all directions.

Closer now. "Ah woooo."

"Hurry! We'll hide behind those boulders," Elm said.

They rushed across the open field and dived behind a boulder, landing in a pile. As he untangled himself, Elm gave a sigh of relief. A low rumble escaped from Sequoia's throat.

Chapter 13

A Rescue

Gigantic wolves, twice the size of a normal wolf, moved into view. Their golden fur had flecks of white intertwined within it. Sequoia glared into the wolves' eyes, then barked. Ignoring the dog, the wolves turned their black muzzles toward the children. Elm swallowed the lump in his throat, then pushed himself between the wolves and Willow. He didn't want to be eaten, but he didn't want to see his sister torn apart, either. Randy jumped to grab the long branches they had used on the devil horses, but they were out of his reach.

As the larger wolf opened his mouth, Elm felt the heat from its breath against his face. He knew this was the end of his journey.

The wolf spoke. "We need your help."

Elm gulped in air. He didn't realize he had been holding his breath. He waited to feel the sharp teeth of the wolf sink into his skin. But they were talking, not attacking. "What? What did you say?"

"You must go on your mission when the half-moon has partly risen. It will give you enough light to see, and the trolls will be sleeping."

Elm's jaw dropped. "What mission?"

"You plan to save the humans. We heard you talking. You must also save the animals." The second wolf's voice was female.

"Why is it our mission? Why can't you save them? We don't know how the three of us can do it," Elm said.

"Not just the three of you. You have a dog," the male wolf said. "And we will help. The trees where the cages hang is on the far side of the trolls' camp. Just remember, don't make a sound. The trolls are light sleepers."

"Easy for you to say—not so easy to do," Randy said. "Why do you want us to help the caged prisoners?"

"The baby wolf is our child," the female said. "The pelts the trolls are wearing are made from the skins of our relatives. There is no love lost between us and the trolls."

"You wouldn't happen to have a few more relatives that would like to help?" Elm said.

"Sorry, no. It's time to rest before the moon is in position." The wolves curled up next to Sequoia.

Two hours passed. The male wolf nudged Elm. "It's time."

Elm awoke to find the wolf sitting next to him. He glanced past the animal into the pitch-black sky and saw twinkling stars. The pale glow from the half-moon gave just enough light to see a few feet in front of him. The wolves told them too much light would wake the trolls, so they couldn't turn on their flashlights.

Elm crawled between Willow and Randy and shook them lightly to wake them.

Randy raised his eyebrows. "Are you sure we have to go?"

"If we're careful, we should be in and out in no time. I don't want to go either, but we must."

"Do you have a plan?" Willow asked.

"Too bad the cages with the people aren't tied with rope like the animals. I'm thinking it will be up to you and me to free the people. You get the boy, and I'll go to the woman, then the man."

"What am I supposed to do?" Randy asked.

"We can't climb the trees holding our weapons, so you will be responsible for the three weapons and our lookout."

"Let's hope we don't need the weapons," Randy said.

"One more question before we go," Willow said. "How are we going to unlock the cages?"

Elm glanced at the wolves. "Do you have an answer to that?"

"While you slept, we slipped into the troll camp and retrieved the keys."

"When were you planning on telling us?" Elm asked.

"When the time was right—humans can be so noisy. At least there are two keys, one for each of you." The wolf handed one to Elm and the other to Willow.

Elm shook his head as he took the key. "Let's go."

They rushed up the hill, lay down, and peeked over the edge. Everything was quiet except for the loud snores from below. Moving down the other side, they stopped and crouched every few feet to ensure none of the trolls had awakened. Once at the bottom, Elm indicated an area for Sequoia and Randy to stand. He and Willow handed over their weapons.

Willow shimmied up the tree. It was hard to tell whether the child was a boy or girl or even the age. Its hair was long and stringy, the skin was pale, and Willow could see the bones through it. Elm moved to the cage holding the woman and turned the key in the lock. The woman looked at him with terror in her eyes.

Elm whispered, "I'm here to help you." He then pointed toward Willow, showing the woman her child was also getting help.

The lady nodded. She crept out of the opening and grasped Elm's hand. The woman wasn't heavy, but the strain of holding her shot pain up his arm. She reached out and grabbed a branch then climbed down the tree. She hurried to where her son and Willow stood.

Elm returned to the tree where the man was caged. He took a deep breath and crawled farther out onto a large branch. Close up, he saw the man had a gaunt face with a long beard. His straggly hair covered one eye. Elm lay on the branch. With one hand holding onto a limb, he stretched his other hand toward the lock. It was just out of his reach. He slid his hand through the bars of the cage and handed the key to the man. The man wiggled the key around the keyhole, unable to get it into the right position. His hands were weak, and the key slipped through his fingers and fell to the ground.

Elm sucked in his breath and held it for a minute. One of the trolls rolled over and farted. The putrid smell permeated the entire area. Randy put his hand over his mouth so he wouldn't gag. Willow pinched her nose between her fingers and moved to where the key had fallen. She tossed it to Elm. He caught it on the first try.

Taking the key from Elm, the man peered up and mouthed the words, "I'm sorry." This time he managed to unlock the cage. He shimmied down the tree by himself.

Elm was about to climb down when he heard a noise above his head. Looking up, he saw a small cage holding hundreds of fairies. He thought it must be the Fairy King and his men. Elm climbed higher. He easily reached the cage and unhooked the latch. The fairies flew up and away. Elm climbed down, satisfied the Fairy Queen would be happy to see her mate.

Once out of the tree, he waved at Willow with hand signals to go back up the hill where the wolves stood watching.

Randy grabbed Elm's arm. "We have to let the animals loose."

"It's too dangerous."

"We can't leave them. We promised the wolves," Randy said.

The rescue was taking longer than Elm thought. He checked the sky. The moon had moved across the sky. In the distance, he could see the beginning of morning twilight. It wouldn't take as long to release the animals as it had the humans. The cages were held by ropes wrapped around the tree for easy access. Almost to the cages, Elm stepped on a twig—snap! To him, it sounded like the shot of a cannonball. He and Randy froze. They couldn't move. One troll sat up, rubbed his eyes, looked around, then lay back down.

Elm and Randy untied the ropes and eased the cages to the ground. They unhooked the latches and opened the doors. The baby wolf joined the large wolves, the rabbits scrambled off into the bushes, and the eagles took flight.

Then everything went wrong.

"I'm going to get some food before we leave." Randy rushed over and grabbed a bucket.

"Leave it." Elm watched Randy dip the bucket into the stew. Randy turned and smiled then tripped over a troll's leg, pouring hot stew over it. The troll roared.

Elm stared in horror as a troll slammed his enormous fist in the middle of Randy's back, sending him flying.

"You're a fool, little wolf," growled the male wolf from halfway up the mountain.

Horrified, Elm watched as the wolf picked up the boy and the woman and threw them on his back. The female wolf slung the man onto her back along with her baby wolf.

"We'll meet you at the base of the waterfall," the male wolf said. Then they rushed up the hill and disappeared.

"Come back. Take us with you," Elm yelled. They had helped the humans and animals escape, and now everyone had abandoned them. *Will we end up in cages?*

Chapter 14

Unexpected Help

Elm stood next to Randy where he was sprawled on the ground. Willow rushed toward them. The campground was full of grunts and snorts as the trolls woke up.

"Where are the humans?" an extra-large troll bellowed. "Catch them! We'll have them for dinner."

Elm grabbed Randy's arm and pulled him up. Willow gathered up the spears and followed them. They sprinted toward the hills with Sequoia in the lead. Weak from hunger, they stumbled several times.

"Where's the invisible wall when you need it?" Willow said.

Five trolls chased them at a distance. Instead of continuing up the hill, where there was nowhere to hide, they circled a grove of trees and raced for a thicket of bushes.

They dived under a thorny hawthorn bush. Exhausted, Elm ignored the long, sharp, white thorns that scratched him. They held their breath and listened. The ground shook as the trolls' giant feet smacked the earth near them.

Sequoia stood next to a tree. Growling and barking, he drew the attention of the trolls away from the bushes.

After the trolls disappeared, Elm felt a stinging sensation in his hands. Thorns stuck out of his fingers, but before he could yank them out, the thorns vanished.

"The thorns!" Elm whispered. "They disappeared into my skin."

Willow nodded. "Mine too."

"Mine didn't." Randy plucked the thorns from his hands.

A small troll crouched down and peered through the bushes. Randy stabbed the troll in its arm, causing it to yelp and alert the others.

The children crawled as fast as possible to get out of the thorny mess, leaving their weapons behind. They raced down a rocky path.

Breathing hard, their pace slowed. Suddenly, several trolls appeared in front of them. Elm twisted around and started sprinting in the opposite direction. Willow and Randy were not far behind him. Elm stopped when he heard Willow cry out. A troll had wrapped a rope around her waist and was dragging her back. The whip of another lasso sounded in the air, wrapping around Randy's legs. A troll jerked the rope, and Randy fell to the ground.

"No!" Elm yelled. "Let them go."

A troll near Elm punched him in his mouth, knocking him to the ground. The pain shot through his head, and blood poured down his chin.

"You didn't think you would get away," the troll said as his mouth curled into a sneer.

The troll grabbed Elm's shirt and tugged him back to his feet, then pushed him in the direction of the camp. Elm staggered over to Willow. They headed toward Randy. Before they could reach him, the troll holding the rope dragged Randy through the dirt and over rocks toward the camp.

Elm and Willow limped along. Whenever they slowed down, the trolls punched them. Several kicked Randy while pulling him over the rough terrain. Others yanked Willow's hair just to hear her cry out. They laughed and imitated her cries.

As they neared the camp, Elm glanced up at the empty cages. He knew it would be their new home at least for a short time.

The trolls threw them in a tent. They were scratched, bruised, and in pain. Elm stumbled and fell. Randy lay in the fetal position, moaning. Willow crawled next to him and put his bleeding head in her lap. Elm moved next to Willow and wrapped his arm around her shoulders.

"Why do you think they put us in a tent instead of the cages?" she asked.

"They think we're too weak to get away, and I'm afraid they don't expect us to be here very long."

"You think they're going to eat us!" she cried. "Where is Sequoia?"

"I hope he's looking for a way to help us," Elm replied as he rubbed his hands together. "My fingers feel strange. There's a burning feeling." He shook his hands and sparks jumped from his fingers.

"Your hands! They're glowing. How did you do that?" Willow asked. "Oh my gosh, my hands are on fire." Sparks flew from her fingers, hitting the back of the tent and singeing a tiny hole in it. "What is going on?"

"I think..." Elm rubbed his jaw where the troll had punched him. "I think it has something to do with the thorns from the hawthorn bush. I remember Grandpa told me a hawthorn has magical power. It symbolizes protection."

"You think the magic from the bush was passed on to us through the thorns that embedded into our fingers?" she asked. "Randy, do you have any magic?"

"No, the thorns didn't go into my hands. I just pulled them out," he replied.

"Give it a try," Willow said.

Randy shook his hands—nothing happened. "I'm not part of your family."

"What?"

"The story your grandpa told. The wizard cursed your family. You can hear the trees talk, and now you have magic," Randy said. "What about the jasper stones? Maybe the trolls will let us go if we trade the stones for our lives."

"Great idea," Elm agreed. "Hey! Anyone out there?"

The guard stomped to the opening. "Huh?"

"We have something to trade for our lives."

The troll checked the area. With no other trolls nearby, he moved into the tent. Elm grabbed his backpack and pulled out his red jasper stone.

"We have three stones. They will bring you good luck. You can have them if you set us free."

The troll grunted. "Let me see."

"Will you let us go?"

The troll had a crazy glimmer in his eyes, then he nodded.

Elm crawled over to the other packs and pulled out the stones. When the troll savagely grabbed Elm's hand, the air crackled and sparks jumped from his fingertips, hitting the troll.

The troll leaped away. "Magic!"

He raised his foot and shoved Elm to the ground, knocking the air out of him. Elm, momentarily paralyzed, dropped the stones. They rolled onto the ground, and the troll took them and lumbered out of the tent. Outside, the troll whistled.

Catching his breath, Elm stepped to the front of the tent and peeked out. Trolls gathered around, staring at the stones. He couldn't understand what they mumbled. It sounded like chaotic gibberish.

The troll with the jasper stones stomped his feet as the others stopped talking. He grunted "magic" and "kill quickly."

"They're going to kill us now," Randy moaned.

"Elm, what are we going to do?" Willow cried.

"I have an idea. Hold my hand. Together we should be able to burn a hole into the back of the tent," Elm explained.

Elm felt a huge surge of power. Pointing, sparks jumped from their hands, and fire burned a hole into the tent.

"We did it," Willow whispered with excitement.

"Hurry, we don't have any time," Elm told Randy. "Hold your breath and jump."

They leaped through the flames, rolled on the ground, then jumped up and ran away from the campground. Spotting Sequoia, they rushed toward him. The dog led them down a path to a small clearing.

"I think we can rest now." Elm sat down. A shadow crossed the trail.

Randy glanced up. "A dragon. Great. We're never going home."

Elm spun around as the ground quaked. Trolls emerged from a tree-lined hill. *We're trapped*, he thought. Trolls on one side of the path and a large beast on the other side.

"What are we going to do?" Willow whimpered.

Sequoia barked, pulled on Elm's pant leg with his teeth, then hurried to the beast.

"Follow Sequoia," Elm said.

Randy murmured. "A dragon. And Sequoia is sitting next to it."

"It's not a dragon. It's a griffin," Elm said.

The enormous beast had the head and wings of an eagle. Its head was covered in beautiful, white feathers. It stared at them with piercing yellow eyes and clicked his hooked beak. Its muscular front legs had sharp talons on the feet. Huge wings folded against its body. The back half of the beast had golden hair with a long tail like a lion. The muscular, hind legs had lion paws. Elm stood in awe of the griffin's beauty even though his brain told him it was dangerous.

"Is it a friend or an enemy?" Willow asked.

The griffin stood up and faced them. It lowered its head, then its body. Sequoia walked up onto its back.

The trolls drew closer.

Elm glanced over his shoulder. "Let's go. Get on the griffin's back."

Willow and Randy had difficulty climbing onto the griffin. Elm saw them slide off several times. The griffin spread its wing from its body to the ground, making it easier to climb. Elm placed his foot on the wing, then felt the heat from a troll's enormous hand as it wrapped around him. It pulled him away from the beast.

Elm's eyes widened as he watched the griffin stretch its long neck, turning its yellow eyes toward the troll. In one quick movement, the griffin's large, sharp beak snapped the troll's arm in half, missing Elm by inches. Elm dropped to the ground, then scrambled onto the griffin's back. The troll screamed in pain as other trolls arrived.

The griffin soared into the sky, and they flew out of troll territory.

Chapter 15

Together Again

Perched on the back of the griffin, Elm held on tight as it soared high into the clouds. Every once in a while, he could see the landscape below. He saw the path, they had left behind. It meandered through grasslands, forests, and even a small desert.

They had been in the air for over an hour. It grew bitterly cold as the temperature dropped so that it was almost unbearable. Everyone, including Sequoia, crawled closer together to keep from freezing.

Elm peeked over the side. Not far away, he saw mountains. "I see it. Didn't the wolves say to meet them at a waterfall?"

Suddenly, the griffin plunged downward. Elm's hand cramped from holding the feathers so tightly.

The griffin circled, getting lower with each loop. Just before coming to a stop, it caught a giant rabbit in its beak. The bunny's screams sounded like a terrified child crying out. Chills ran down Elm's spine.

Once firmly on the ground, Elm and the others slid off its back. They heard a crack, and the rabbit went quiet. The griffin lay down and ate its prey. They raced away from the griffin, hoping it would not make them part of its meal.

"I smell food cooking." Randy sniffed the air.

"That's what got us in trouble last time," Elm said.

They crept toward smoke wafting into the air. The sound of wings flapping made Elm look over his shoulder. The griffin, finished with its dinner, flew into the air and out of sight.

Rounding a curve, Elm saw a waterfall splashing into a lake. Not far from the water and next to a crackling fire lay the two wolves and their baby. The man, woman, and child leaned against them. Skewers above the flames held several animals cooking.

Elm whispered in Willow's ear, "We're safe."

Willow tilted her face as tears filled her eyes. "Let's go be with humans." She smiled back at him.

The three of them hurried forward.

"You made it!" The little boy yelled with delight. He met them halfway and hugged each of them, then petted Sequoia.

The man greeted them with a handshake. "Thanks for saving my family."

"Who are you?" Elm asked.

"The Miller family. We lived next door to you. You look the same as the last time we saw you."

"You must be Jacob." Willow said to the small boy.

He nodded.

Mrs. Miller took the spit off the fire and placed food on the ground. "You must be starving. Please, come eat."

"Tell us how you escaped from the trolls. We were angry at the wolves for leaving you behind, but they assured us you would survive," Mr. Miller said.

Randy, thinking of his stomach, replied, "Let's eat. We can talk later."

Mr. Miller laughed, put an arm around Randy, and together they walked toward the fire. As they ate, Elm told most of the story of their escape.

"How long were you in the cages?" Willow asked.

"It seemed like months," Mrs. Miller said. "I don't think my son would have lasted much longer. The trolls gave us just enough food to keep us alive."

"I thought trolls ate people," Randy said.

"They do, but they had plenty of animals available, so they were saving us until the food was scarce," Mr. Miller replied. "I'm guessing no one is looking for us anymore since we've been missing for years."

"Years? No, you've only been gone for six months," Elm said.

"We've been tracking the days," Mrs. Miller said. "We've calculated at least three years."

Elm and Willow exchanged looks.

"Uh, this is Randy. He lives in the house where you lived," Willow said. Randy waved and kept stuffing his mouth. "His family moved there a month ago. Your family and the town's people searched for you for months after you disappeared. When no was able to locate you after three months, they decided you had moved away."

The male wolf interrupted the conversation. "You've been through a lot today. When you're finished eating, you need to rest. We'll camp here for a few days. There's plenty of food and water. You need to regain some strength before you continue your journey up the boulders beside the waterfall."

Elm yawned. "Do you know the way to our home?"

"You still have a long trip," the male wolf replied.

Elm didn't completely trust the wolves since they had run off and left them behind with the trolls, but for some reason, he felt safe. Full of food, tired, and aching all over, he lay down. As he drifted off to sleep, he saw Sequoia snuggled next Jacob. Elm smiled, then fell asleep.

Chapter 16

Training

The next few days kept everyone busy. The female wolf took Elm and Willow a distance from their camp where they could practice controlling the fire that came from their fingers.

"Making fire is a part of magic. Does that make us wizards or witches?" Elm asked.

"No," the she-wolf replied.

"Will we have this power when we're home?" Willow asked.

"I doubt it. I've never been where you come from, so I don't know."

"I wish you could come home with us," Willow said.

"Enough chit-chat. It's time for you to practice."

"I don't understand why we have to practice." Elm raised his arms toward a pile of rocks. A few sparks jumped from his fingers, but the rocks didn't move.

Willow aimed her fingers at a pile of dead leaves. Bright flames shot across the opening and set them on fire.

"How did you do that?" Elm asked.

"I don't know," she replied.

"You are too impatient. You must learn control along with concentration. Without control, you place your compadres in danger," the wolf said to Elm.

Elm held out his hand. The only thing on his mind was rocks—fire. He said the words over silently in his mind. He pointed his fingers—his hand felt a surge of heat, then sparks shot forward, blowing the pile of rocks in all directions.

"Woohoo, I did it!" He gave Willow a thumbs up.

"Keep practicing," the wolf said. "I'm going to check on the baby and little boy."

Elm and Willow continued to practice, improving with each try.

"I want to try something." Willow took Elm's hand. "Hold my hand, and let's see if we can move that medium-size boulder with fire."

They raised their hands toward the boulder. Fire shot from their fingers. The boulder didn't move but exploded into a hundred pieces.

"Holy smokes!" Elm said. "That was amazing. Together we're invincible."

"Don't get too cocky. But I do wish we had known this when we were fighting the trolls. We could have blown them away." Willow chuckled.

****

The Miller family searched for sturdy branches and used stones to sharpen the ends of the limbs into spears. They practiced jabbing by thrusting the spear from their side to an upward position. They also tried throwing the spears at large pine cones sitting on top of a boulder. They held the spear, next to their ear and tossed it like they were throwing a dart. Each day they improved.

The male wolf took Randy to a secluded area and trained him—on what, no one knew. When Randy returned from training, everyone noticed his confidence growing. He stood taller. He didn't jump when an unexpected noise was heard. When he was not with the wolf, he ran laps around the campground. Sometimes he took Sequoia with him, and they would run for hours and return exhausted. The wolf always called Randy "little wolf," never by his name. Randy howled when he said it.

The next few days, they continued to master their training.

****

Days later, Elm watched as the female wolf prepared nuts and berries for breakfast.

"The Millers can now catch food with their spears or they can use them as weapons," the she-wolf said as everyone gathered together to eat. "Randy can run at the speed of a wolf, and if needed, surprise an enemy from behind. You two have improved with your fire-magic, and it will continue to get better as you practice along the way. Today, everyone will continue to practice. Tonight, you will rest, and tomorrow, you will travel."

"Do you know what kind of monsters we'll have to fight?" Willow asked.

"If luck is with you, you may not see any. Though you will be traveling through strange territories."

"You need to know how to fight. You also need the strength to travel through the rough terrain you're about to encounter," the male wolf said.

"Will you travel with us?" Elm asked.

"No."

After a full day of training, everyone was exhausted and headed for bed. Eyes closed and nearly asleep, Elm felt something rough coil around his legs. It slowly crossed over his body, pinning him to the ground. He opened his mouth to call for help—no sound escaped. The smell of dirt and wood filled his nose. He recognized the smell—the sickening scent of tree roots. He couldn't breathe. The root was squeezing the life out of him. Rising in front of Elm's face, the root resembled a snake poised to strike him.

"You think you have friends to protect you and magic to save you. I, too, have many friends at my beck and call. You'll never make it home."

Elm jumped up and looked around—no trees or roots. Everyone else lay asleep. *Just a dream. Or was it?*

Chapter 17

Birds, Bats, and Snakes, Oh No

The light of dawn woke Elm. He stepped over Willow, then wandered around the grounds. The campfire had died in the night. He discovered the wolves were gone. Still feeling sluggish, he was in no hurry to continue the journey, so he sat and waited for the others to wake. He leaned against a tree, closed his eyes, and wondered why his parents had never told him and his sister about the history of their family.

"Elm, what are you doing?" Willow shook his shoulder.

He tilted his head and looked at her quizzically. He was surprised he hadn't heard her approach. Blinking, he realized everyone was awake.

"I woke up early. I guess I fell back asleep." he said. "The wolves are gone." Elm didn't tell anyone about his dream.

"That means our training is over, and we can continue to find our way home," Randy said. "I'm ready to hit the road."

The Miller family nodded in agreement.

"We should have meat for days before we'll need to hunt again," Mr. Miller said.

Mrs. Miller rolled the cooked food in leaves to keep it from spoiling. Randy placed items into his backpack. Willow kicked the dirt with her foot as she kept her eyes on the ground.

"Did you lose something?" Elm asked.

She bent over and picked up a stick that had fallen from a willow tree. It was about twelve inches long and pointed at one end.

"What's that?" Elm asked.

"It's going to be my wand." She held the stick and waved it around in the air.

"Wand? Magic comes from your fingers."

"True, but I still want a wand. Watch this." She held the stick in her palm, stretching her thumb and fingers out along the stick. She winked at Jacob. She waved her hand and aimed at a small rock. Sparks jumped from her fingers, moved down the stick, and hit the rock.

Everyone laughed. Their spirits were high with the anticipation of nearing the end of their journey.

Elm studied the mountain they were about to hike. He had never climbed before, but the way the rocks were set, it didn't look as if it would be very difficult. It resembled a climbing wall with a few ledges to stand on. The only problem he saw was the rocks were wet and probably slippery.

Elm pulled a rope from his pack. "I think it's time to use this," he said. "It's not long enough to tie around everyone, but we can hold it as we climb so we don't fall."

"Do you have a plan?" Willow asked.

Everyone turned their attention to him. Elm wondered. *When did I become the leader of this band of lost?*

"Randy will lead," Elm said.

Randy raised an eyebrow. "What? Why me?"

"Even though you don't want to admit it, you have a secret power."

"I don't have any powers. You should lead. You have magic, which will come in handy if we encounter any more monsters."

"Monsters?" Jacob whined.

"No, no, no," Randy said as he knelt next to Jacob. "I was just trying to get Elm to go first."

"No monsters?" Jacob smiled.

"You got it J-boy." Randy hugged the boy.

Jacob giggled. "You and the wolves like to use nicknames."

"You don't want to be called J-boy?" Randy asked.

"Yeah, I like it. Why did the wolves call you 'little wolf?'"

"Not sure. My last name is Wolff. I guess that's why."

"Come on, Randy, you know why they called you that." Elm laughed.

"Shut up," Randy said, growling.

Ignoring Randy, Elm said, "Back to the lineup. Randy first because he has great hearing and sense of smell. Then Jacob, Mr. and Mrs. Miller, and Willow, and I'll be last. We'll tie the rope around Randy and just wrap it around everyone else."

"I don't think I can do it. It's too high," Jacob whimpered.

Mr. Miller patted his son on his head. "You can do it. And we're all here to help you."

With all their belongings packed, they began a slow climb. It was more like a crawl. Randy reached from rock to rock. Some crumbled in his hand, making him stumble. Other times, his foot slipped on wet stones. He never glanced back afraid he would lose his nerve to continue.

He called over his shoulder, "Watch your step. The rocks are slippery."

They had not climbed very far when Jacob's feet flew off the rocks, and he let go of the rope. Sliding down the waterfall, he was swept into the lake below.

Mrs. Miller screamed.

Elm and Sequoia jumped into the waterfall and slid down the smooth granite wall to the lake. The others scrambled back down the mountain and waited at the shoreline.

Elm surfaced, coughing and gasping for air. He was still under the waterfall, and the power of the falls tried to push him back under. His only thought was of Jacob. He caught a breath of air and sank back under the water. He did several breaststrokes and moved away from the turbulence of the falls.

Coming up for more air, he searched the area but didn't see Jacob. He ducked under the water. Coming back up one more time, he watched as Sequoia swam to a small whirlpool. Elm saw a head bobbing above the water. He swam as hard as he could to Jacob and helped him climb onto Sequoia's back. Together, they moved to the shore, then Elm collapsed. Jacob climbed off Sequoia and sat down.

Crying, Mrs. Miller hugged Jacob. "Are you all right?"

After coughing up water, Jacob smiled. "It was like a ride at the park, except without a boat."

Willow knelt next to Elm. "You're a hero."

"No, I'm not. I just happened to be the first one to jump in the water," he replied.

Everyone gathered around Elm and Sequoia, thanking them, hugging them, and making a big fuss. *I don't want to be a leader or a hero. I just want to be a kid at home playing.*

They delayed their climb until Elm and Jacob had time to recover.

"Let's put J-boy in front of me with the rope tied around him and me," Randy said. "That way, I can make sure he doesn't slip away." He looked at Mr. Miller.

"Yes, of course. I trust you to take care of him," Mr. Miller replied.

They started up the side of the waterfall. Again, they encountered crumbling rocks and slippery stones, but they were able to continue without anyone falling. The higher they climbed the farther they were from the waterfall. The splashing water didn't hit the rocks.

Unexpectedly, the sky turned from bright daylight to complete darkness. Elm glanced up and saw spots before his eyes. Once he focused, he saw hundreds of crows, as large as condors, hovering above them. The sound was excruciating. All the crows cawed at the same time. One flew nearby and plucked a fox from a hole and carried it off.

Several of the larger crows zoomed across the sky and dive bombed toward the climbers. Mr. Miller pulled his spear from his pack and stabbed at the birds.

A crow screeched from its injury. The other birds let out a loud raspy "caw, caw." Their flight became a frenzy of blackness, which mesmerized the climbers.

113

Elm held onto a rock as he stretched backward, looking up. "Randy, I see an opening. Hurry! Move."

Climbing twenty more feet, Randy pushed Jacob into a hole, then jumped in it. The crows lowered their heads and flew directly at Mr. Miller.

Willow raised her wand. Sparks jumped from her fingers, raced down the wand, and into the sky. The birds soared upward.

Mr. Miller made it to the opening, followed by his wife, then Willow, and Sequoia. Before Elm entered, he turned and focused on the blackness. He extended his arm and pointed his fingers. Flames shot into the sky. The birds were fast—they split apart and the fire soared right past them. Elm climbed into the hole.

They were surrounded by light. Crystals in the walls reflected colors of blue and white. It was fascinating and mysterious at the same time. The ceiling was high like a cathedral and had tiny holes. In the distance, a small waterfall flowed into a narrow lake.

Elm yelled, "Hurry! The crows are right behind me."

A gigantic crow flew into the cave. Elm hit the bird with sparks from his fingers. The bird fell to the floor.

"Find something to block the hole!" Mrs. Miller cried.

Elm and Willow crouched at the opening. Sparks shot from their fingers, causing the crows to hesitate. Randy and Mr. Miller gathered as many stones as they could find and piled them against the opening. They waited, listening, but no longer heard the crows.

"That was close." Mr. Miller wiped the sweat dripping from his forehead. He sat down and leaned against the wall. "Did you know a flock of crows is called a murder of crows?"

"I think those birds had murder on their mind," Randy said.

"Daddy, look. Is that a vampire's cave?" Jacob whimpered. Huge stalactites loomed overhead on each side of the opening, like a mouth with razor-sharp fangs.

"No, son. It's just a formation caused by water dripping," Mr. Miller replied.

"Let's hope that's all it is, though I wouldn't be surprised considering everything else we've encountered," Willow said.

A rustling sound came from deep inside the tunnel. The dog barked and bolted into the opening.

"Sequoia, come back," Elm yelled as the dog barked wildly.

The noise grew louder and closer. Everyone moved away from the tunnel's entrance. Elm peered in, when *whoosh*, thousands of bats flew over his head and out tiny holes above. The bats

115

squealed as the crows caught them, causing Jacob to put his hands over his ears.

Mrs. Miller placed her arm around him. "Do you think it's safe?" she asked her husband.

"Yes," he replied.

"Before we continue, let's have some food," Willow suggested.

They ate cold, grilled rabbit and drank fresh water from the lake.

Elm ate slowly, his mind wandering. *What was waiting for them in the mountain's tunnels?*

Chapter 18

Etchings on the Wall

Elm rubbed the back of his neck as he entered a passageway. Semi-darkness surrounded him. Willow turned on her flashlight. Elm noticed black dents along the dingy walls, making the hair on the back of his neck tingle. He jerked his head around. He could have sworn he saw a black spot open like an eye. *Is the tree still tracking our every move? Should I tell the others? No, it would only frighten them, and everyone is already scared.*

"Which way?" Randy asked.

Elm glanced from one passageway to another. "This one looks like it has a slight incline. Maybe it will lead to the top of the mountain."

"At least there aren't any tree roots or crows in here," Mrs. Miller said.

Elm didn't respond. He only stared at the ground. He sensed there would be more trouble, even if he couldn't see it.

Willow drew near him and looked into his eyes. "Is anything wrong?" Even though she whispered, her voice echoed and everyone heard.

"Elm?" Mr. Miller said with concern.

"No, nothing's wrong. I'm just tired. I want to go home. Soon."

They trudged a short distance through the tunnel and entered a smaller cave.

"Check out this painting, um, drawing," Randy said.

Lifelike carvings of crows, snakes, and other strange animals lined the crystal walls. Light shining from above shimmered, making it look as if they moved.

"What is this? Do you think it's real?" Willow bit her lip as she placed her hands over a carving of a snake with feathers on its head. "I hope it doesn't live in these tunnels."

Elm glanced at it. Of all the impossible things they had encountered, now this. He had seen a show on television about a feathered serpent. It was a god to the Aztecs. Why would it be here, hundreds of miles from Mexico?

They crept along the slick, limestone floors. Elm stepped over several deep holes, which appeared to be endless. Jacob dropped a medium-sized rock into one of them. Elm never heard it hit bottom.

"Strange. I didn't think we had climbed very high," Randy said.

"Nothing underground is what it seems to be," Willow replied.

A dark shadow crossed Elm's path. Unsure of what was ahead, he came to a complete stop.

"Why did you stop?" Randy asked.

Elm placed his finger to his lips. "Shh."

They stood in silence for a moment. A dry, raspy hissing vibrated through the tunnel, then a snake's tail rattled. Thousands of mice, lizards, and other creatures scurried past them. Elm was shocked. They hadn't traveled very far before encountering another obstacle.

"Ugh, that's not a good sign." Willow squealed and jumped out of the way.

For a second Elm paused, then yelled, "Go back."

They ran, dodging holes. Elm shivered as he noticed several rats huddled together in a small concave.

Back in the small chamber, they had just left, Jacob pointed. "The wall—the picture is missing."

Bewildered, Elm moved his fingers over the space where the carving of the snake had been. "The shadow. It was the snake from the wall."

"That's impossible," Randy said.

The noise of a snake's rattler reverberated off the walls of the tunnel.

"Hurry! This way," Elm said.

They sprinted out of the chamber and up the corridor. The hissing of the snake grew fainter.

Eventually, Elm didn't hear the snake at all. After several hours, Elm felt a strong gust of wind. Running ahead, he saw light pouring into the tunnel from an opening. He walked onto a covered ledge shaped like a horseshoe.

Elm glanced up the side of the mountain. He stretched his arms and sucked in fresh air. "This looks like a great spot to take a break before we have to climb again."

"No birds. No snakes." Willow smiled. "Taking a break sounds good to me."

"Me too," Jacob said.

Elm pulled the rope from his backpack. "We better use this for safety."

They wrapped the rope around each other.

"I didn't realize how exhausted I am," Mr. Miller said.

They arranged themselves on the ledge. Mr. and Mrs. Miller lay next to the opening, Jacob beside them. Willow settled on one side of the ledge against the wall, with Randy on the other side, and Elm and Sequoia in the middle. It didn't take long for everyone to fall asleep.

Elm awoke to the sound of hissing. When he opened his eyes, a large snake's head peered down at him. Elm sucked in his breath and closed his eyes to small slits. *If he thinks I'm asleep, maybe—just maybe—the snake will crawl away.* He watched through his eyelashes as a forked tongue flicked out of the snake. Elm tried to cry out for help—he had no voice. The snake wrapped its body around Elm, crushing the air out of him, then plunged over the ledge. Falling, the rope around his waist yanked, waking everyone.

"Awwwwwww!" Elm knew he was falling to his death. He gasped, then heard Randy's voice.

"Everyone, hold the rope."

Randy's arm reached over the edge. The rope jerked as it tightened around Elm's waist, and he dangled in the air as Randy hoisted him up.

Back on the ledge, he slid down, breathless, and wrapped his arms around his legs. "Where's the snake?"

"There's no snake. You were dreaming." Willow sat next to Elm. Tears streamed down her face.

"I'm sorry I scared everyone." Elm's breath hitched in his throat.

"Are you okay?" Mrs. Miller asked.

"Yes, just a little shaken," Elm said. "I'd like to rest a little longer before we start climbing. I need to get my nerves under control."

They settled down on the ledge for another hour. Willow and Randy told the Millers about the map. How it was divided into different areas, and they should be getting closer to home. Elm half-listened to the conversation while thinking of the nightmares he'd been having. *Were they just bad dreams or premonitions? If I remembered the map correctly, we have one more area to travel through. The Land of Who. What does that even mean?*

Elm rubbed Sequoia's ears, then he stood up. "Thank you for saving me. I feel better now if you want to continue."

They gathered their belongings, and Randy and Jacob led the rest of them on the climb. Willow and Elm brought up the end. Stepping stones led to the top. The climb turned out to be easier than he thought.

"Yay! Back on flat land," Randy said.

Elm thought, *Yeah, it's flat, but the sun's blazing hot.* He saw heat waves shimmering off the ground. In the distance were trees.

With every step Elm took, the trees in the distance seemed to get farther away.

Randy squinted his eyes. "Those trees are moving."

Chapter 19

Who Are You?

"How can trees walk?" Jacob blinked at Randy, who shrugged his shoulders.

After hours of walking in the hot sun, Elm's legs began to cramp, and he had a light headache. Sweat evaporated as soon as it beaded on his skin. Dust covered everyone's face. He knew they needed to find shade soon, or they would all suffer from heat exhaustion, something his father had warned him about many times since they live in the South.

Finally reaching the tree line, they collapsed in the shade. Willow passed around bottles of water. As they rested, they scanned the new area. Before them stood trees of all sizes and species, some familiar, others foreign to this part of the world. No birds chirped. No squirrels jumped from branch to branch. There was no sound of any kind. Even though a light breeze filled the air, the leaves didn't move.

"I think we're in a walking forest," Elm said. Everyone looked at him. "Remember, Willow? Dad told us about these trees."

"I don't remember."

Elm pointed at a grove of palm trees. "Those trees are Socratea Exorrhiza. They're found in Ecuador. They move across the forest as new roots relocate them. They are always searching for more sunlight."

Facing another group of trees, Elm said, "Those are called Jinmenju. They grow in the mountains of Japan."

"Do they walk?" Jacob asked.

Elm laughed. "No, they have fruit with human faces. When you walk past them, the faces laugh at you."

"I've never heard of anything like that before," Mr. Miller said.

"Those." Elm indicated another group of trees. "We'll need to keep our distance. They're called lotus trees. I don't recall the legend, but for some reason, I think it's dangerous to get near them."

"You mean lotus flower?" Mrs. Miller asked.

"No, it's a tree."

"Will any of these trees attack us?" Willow asked.

"They shouldn't unless they're under the control of the live oak tree. Is everyone ready to cross the forest?"

They nodded.

"Let's hold hands," Willow suggested.

Elm went first, then Willow, Jacob, the Millers, and Randy last. As they passed the Jinmenju, the fruit made faces and giggled.

Holding Willow's hand as they walked past the laughing fruit, Elm said, "Ignore the fruit. It can't hurt you, but we need to get to those pine trees."

Elm felt Willow's hand let go of his. He turned to ask why and found he stood alone.

The palm trees shuffled across the path, blocking his view.

He yelled, "Willow! Randy! Where are you?"

No answer. He noticed shadows moving on the other side of the palms. He ran, squeezing through a small opening. Everyone had scattered throughout the trees.

Sequoia barked. Elm found himself outside the tree line where Jacob lay on the ground. His eyes rolled back in his head, and he was babbling.

"Mrs. Miller, there's something wrong with Jacob," Elm cried out as he cradled Jacob in his lap.

"With who?"

"Your son."

"I don't have a son."

"Willow!" Elm yelled.

"What?" she replied, unconcerned.

"Something's wrong with Jacob. Willow, are you listening to me?"

She giggled. "Who is that boy standing over there? He's cute."

"It's Randy. Is there something wrong with your eyesight?" Elm asked.

"That name sounds familiar. Do we know him?"

"Oh my gosh! What is going on?" Elm still had Jacob in his lap. "Randy!"

Randy turned, and Elm waved him over.

"I think I'm lost. Can you help me?" Randy asked.

"Sure," Elm replied. "Have a seat. Do you mind holding this little boy in your lap while I gather everyone else together?"

Elm placed Jacob in Randy's lap. Sequoia lay down. Willow walked next to them. Elm moved back into the trees and found Mr. and Mrs. Miller near the lotus tree playing hide and seek.

"Mr. Miller!" Elm called.

"Do you want to play?" Mr. Miller replied.

"Sure, can we talk first?"

"You're no fun." He giggled like a child.

"Before we play, I want you to meet my friends. The more the merrier, right?" Elm said.

Mrs. Miller looked over her shoulder. "More kids. Let's go!" She clapped her hands together.

The three of them joined Willow, Randy, and Jacob.

"Now I remember why we shouldn't go near the lotus tree. Did you eat any of the fruit from the tree?" Elm asked.

"Fruit? I didn't eat any. By the way, I'm starved. Do we have anything to eat?" Willow said.

"Did any of you eat the fruit?"

They shook their heads with their eyes downcast.

"Yes, you did. The legend is, if you eat fruit from the lotus tree, you will forget everything that is important to you."

They all started talking at the same time.

"I'm hungry."

"Let's eat."

"I'm thirsty."

"Okay, okay. Wait a minute." Elm pulled food from Mrs. Miller's sack and water from his own and passed it around to everyone.

They gobbled it like they hadn't eaten in days and sucked up the water. Even Jacob, who had recovered, took a few bites. Elm kept his eyes on everyone else as he ate.

Willow crossed her arms and frowned. "What are we waiting for? When are we going into the woods?"

"Yeah, if we stop every time you want to rest or eat, we're never going to get home," Randy added.

"Mommy," Jacob said.

"Yes, hon?" she replied.

"I want to go home."

"Do you know who you are?" Elm asked.

"What are you talking about? Of course, we know who we are," Willow said.

"You didn't half an hour ago."

They stared at him, confused. He relayed what had happened. None of them remembered anything.

Chapter 20

Trees

They reentered the forest for the second time, not single file, but as a group with the rope wrapped around them—more like two by two, with Mr. and Mrs. Miller in the lead, then Randy and Willow. Elm held Jacob's hand, and everyone held onto the rope.

Elm knew the trees watched him. They had watched him ever since he had been dragged underground. The hairs on his neck prickled.

"Oh, look!" Mrs. Miller said. "Fruit for dessert." She and her husband moved toward the lotus tree.

128

Elm called out, "We can't eat the fruit. It's poison."

Disappointed, the Millers turned back to the path. After what seemed like half a mile, the ground vibrated. The sound of wood cracking filled the air. Trees pulled their roots from the ground, making a loud, sucking noise. They moved almost in formation. Hundreds of trees gathered and communicated with each other in a strange language.

"Can you understand them?" Elm asked Willow. She shook her head.

One of the larger trees yelled, "Get them!"

The trees rushed toward them.

Elm felt the rope go limp in his hand. "Don't run! Wait! We need to stay together! We can fight as a team."

No one listened. Everyone took off in a different direction.

A thin branch wrapped around Elm and squeezed. He winced in pain and tried to catch his breath. The more he struggled, the tighter it gripped him. He brought his hand down hard against the branch. All his thoughts went to burning the tree. He felt the power surge into his fingers. Sparks shot from his fingertips and set the branch on fire. A shriek of pain came from the tree, and it loosened its grip.

Gnarled branches reached toward Willow. She backed away, stumbling over roots, and crashed to the ground. Elm scrambled to his feet. His heart skipped a beat, then he rushed over to help her.

"Are you hurt?" he asked.

"No. Where is everyone?"

"They scattered. Everywhere."

Elm's skin crawled as he heard a scream. Not any scream—one from a child. As he and everyone else rushed toward Jacob, they stopped and watched in horror. The trees tossed Jacob from one to another, like a ball. He was at least fifteen feet in the air.

"Mom!" Jacob screamed at the top of his lungs.

Mrs. Miller shrieked.

With surprising agility, Mr. Miller snatched up his spear and charged. He stabbed the trunks of the trees repeatedly. A split second later, a tree swung its large branch against Mr. Miller and knocked him into the air. He landed with a thump and lay semiconscious on his back. Mrs. Miller crept to her husband.

A swift wind picked up leaves, making them swirl into a whirlwind. Elm lost sight of Jacob. He ducked as branches swooped past his head. The trees tried to stop him from reaching Willow. He was close enough, so he grabbed her hand.

"Put the boy down, or we will set you on fire."

"We'll burn this whole forest," Willow cried. "You'll never walk again."

The tree holding Jacob placed him on the ground, then backed away. A palm tree moved with such speed Willow didn't have time to move out of its way. The palm slapped her in the face with its sharp frond. Blood poured from her cheek.

"No!" Elm yelled. He raised his fingers toward the palm. Sparks sprang from the tips, singeing the fronds.

All the trees moved away, only to regroup. While the trees collaborated on their new strategy, a weeping willow called to Elm, "Hurry, come under my branches."

"How can we trust you?" He saw the other trees shuffling in their direction.

"You need a place to hide," the willow tree continued. "You have no choice except to trust me."

Willow and the others hurried under the branches. The tree said again, "Run, Elm, or you won't make it home."

He glared at the tree, then moved under the limbs. The willow draped its branches to the ground, like a green waterfall.

"Willow," the tree said, "take a few of my leaves and place them on your cheek. They will stop the bleeding."

She gently pulled a couple of leaves from a branch and held them to her face. "It feels cool. There's no pain." She removed the leaves from her face.

"It's healed. There's not even a scar," Elm said. "Here come the trees."

Hidden beneath the willow branches, Elm and the others watched the trees search the area. The wind whistled loudly through the leaves as the trees moved. It reminded Elm of the sound of a train. The palms grouped together and used their roots like tentacles along the ground, feeling for a human body.

The Jinmenju trees stood near the willow. The faces on the fruit turned into sneers. Drool dripped from their mouths. The eyes jerked from one direction to another. All at once, the faces turned toward the willow, then just as quickly turned away. The tree moved away.

"That was close," Randy said.

"You're almost to the portal you've been seeking," the willow replied.

"Where is it?" Mrs. Miller asked.

The willow raised its branches and pointed in the distance.

"Thanks." Willow hugged the tree's big trunk.

"I will always save one of my own. Since your name is Willow, it makes you part of our family. Now, hurry before the other trees return."

"How will we know when we reach the portal?" Elm asked.

"You'll know."

They gathered their packs. Scanning the area before they left the safety of the willow tree, Elm said, "Run as fast as you can, and don't stop for anything."

As everyone scurried across the open land, Elm had an uneasy feeling. He noticed one lonely tree covered in kudzu vines. Suddenly, its limbs moved.

Elm yelled, "Run!"

Willow ran through an invisible wall, then Randy, Elm, Jacob, and Mrs. Miller.

"I'll never get used to that." Willow stopped mid-sentence and her eyes widened.

"Ugh! Slime," Randy grumbled.

"Welcome home." The live oak tree stood in front of them.

"Home? We're home?" Randy yelled.

"Where's Daddy?" Jacob asked.

Elm turned and watched the lonely tree use the vines as a lasso. It threw the lasso, coiling around Mr. Miller and knocking him to the ground. The tree dragged him back into the forest. Elm's heart dropped. He knew he couldn't leave Mr. Miller behind. He would have to go back through the portal.

"We have to go back!" Mrs. Miller cried.

"No! You, Jacob, and Willow stay here. You'll be safe. Randy and I will go back."

"I want to go," Willow argued.

"Not this time," Elm replied. "Someone needs to make it back to Mom and Dad."

133

Elm and Randy stepped back through the invisible wall, and Willow tried to follow. The barrier closed.

Elm ran to the willow tree. "Where did they take the man?"

"You don't have time. The portal will close soon."

"We can't leave without him. Which way should we go?"

The willow tree pointed at several trees standing together. "Just past them, you will find the man. You must hurry."

Elm glanced back. The web-like wall shimmered, then everyone's image faded from view.

"We have to get back home. Why don't you set the trees on fire?" Randy whispered.

"No," Elm said. "Until we can see Mr. Miller—I can't start a fire."

They neared the edge of the trees. Elm pointed. Mr. Miller was on the ground, moaning in pain. The fruit heads turned toward them and started chattering.

The trees lunged at them. Elm raised both his hands and sparks shot out. The trees stood still for a moment.

"I have an idea," Elm whispered. "Get the trees to chase you."

Randy's eyes widened. "What?"

"You can outrun those trees. If you get them to follow you, I'll get Mr. Miller. Once we're back together, I'll use my fire to keep the trees away."

Elm rushed back to the willow tree and hid. Randy let out a howl, then ran in the opposite direction. The trees chased him.

Elm hurried to Mr. Miller. He jerked at the vines, but they wouldn't release their hold. He finally used sparks from his fingers to singe them. The vines loosened, and Elm untangled them. He then helped Mr. Miller up. Supporting him, they hurried to the portal.

"Randy!" Elm yelled. "Come now! Hurry!"

Randy sprinted, the other trees following him. When he passed the willow tree, it moved to block the path of the trees.

"Thanks, Mr. Willow!" Randy yelled.

Together, they hurried to the portal, but they hit a wall and bounced off.

"No!" Randy yelled, grabbing his head in frustration. "I want to go home."

"Look," Mr. Miller said. There was a small opening in the lower edge of the portal.

They crawled, Mr. Miller first, then Randy.

Elm had almost made it through when his foot would not move. Randy grabbed one of his arms while Mr. Miller grabbed the other, together they pulled with all their strength. Elm felt the portal close around him. He was almost through except his right foot. It was caught between worlds. He placed his free foot against an invisible wall and pushed. A loud pop was heard as his foot came through the closing portal. He immediately felt throbbing pain. He rolled on the ground, pulling his knee to his chest.

"My foot! The pain," Elm cried.

Everyone gathered around him. Mrs. Miller took Elm's shoe off and felt his foot. Elm squeezed his fist together, trying not to cry out in agony.

"I'm not a doctor, but I don't think it's broken. But it is very badly bruised, and it looks like your big toe is broken." She moved next to her husband.

The live oak tree laughed. No one heard it except Elm and Willow.

Elm wiped a tear from his face. "I'm going to set you on fire."

Willow knelt beside Elm, then pointed her wand at the tree. Nothing happened. "We lost our magic."

"Let's go home. My family will be wondering what's happened to me," Randy said.

"Help me up, please," Elm said.

Willow and Randy pulled Elm up. He looked at the live oak tree and noticed the hole they had entered at the beginning of their journey was no longer there. He faced the other way then took a deep breath.

"The portals are gone."

Suddenly, a blustery wind stirred fallen leaves into a frenzy. They blew up into the air and surrounded the Miller family. The wind stopped as quickly as it started. The leaves fell to the ground.

Tears welled up in Mrs. Miller's eyes. "I'm so thankful you found us. We have been wandering these woods for months." Her eyes darted back and forth as she wrung her hands. "Just look at our clothes. They have turned to rags."

"Yeah. It's no fun eating worms, bugs, and berries." Jacob sniffled.

Mr. Miller put his arm around his wife then looked at Elm. "Thank you. I don't think we could have survived much longer. Every time we thought we found the way out, trees seemed to blocked our way. It was very confusing."

Elm stared at the Millers in disbelief.

"What about everything that happened?" Elm asked.

"What?" Mr. Miller asked.

"The underground, the trolls, the walking trees," Elm said.

Mr. Miller shook his head. "Have you been dreaming?"

It didn't make any sense. *How could they have forgotten everything?* Elm wondered.

Willow squeezed his arm. "We no longer have magic, but the trees around us do. The leaves—they must have caused the Millers to lose their memory. Randy, do you remember what happened to us?"

"Do I! Sure. And I want to get the heck out of these woods," he said.

In the distance, Elm heard his parents calling their names.

Chapter 21

Home

"Elm! Willow!" Elm heard his mom scream at the top of her lungs.

"Randy!" Mr. Underwood yelled.

Suddenly, Sequoia ran out of the bushes.

"Hey, boy, where are the children?" Mrs. Underwood asked as she knelt down to the dog.

"Mom!" Elm and Willow shouted.

Through the forest came Randy and Willow, walking with their arms around Elm as he hobbled.

"What happened to you?" Elm's mom asked.

"I somehow bruised my foot, and my toe is broken," Elm said.

Randy interrupted the conversation, asking, "Where are my parents?"

"They're still at your grandparents' house."

"What?" His eyes widened and his smile faded. "They didn't come to look for me?"

"Look for you? You've been gone a half-day."

Randy's mouth fell open. The children, confused, exchanged glances.

Mrs. Underwood's eyes flashed with anger. "You went into the forest, and you know better." She stared at Elm and Willow. "You two are grounded for the rest of—"

The Miller family came through the underbrush.

The scolding came to a halt. Mrs. Underwood rubbed her eyes. "Oh my gosh! You found the Millers. How? Where? You're heroes!" She rushed to Mrs. Miller. "Let's get you to the house."

That was all they needed to hear. Willow and Randy headed to the house, and Mr. Underwood carried Elm.

Sitting in the living room, Elm shook his head in disbelief. "A half a day. We've been gone only half a day."

"My parents didn't even know I was missing." Randy laughed. "I'm so happy to be back home."

Elm listened as his mom talked to the Millers. She buzzed around them like a bee around flowers. "We're so glad you're alive. How did you survive all this time?"

"May I use your phone to call our parents?" Mr. Miller asked.

"Sure, the phone is in the kitchen," she replied.

Exhausted, Mrs. Miller sat down and laid her head on the table.

"Oh, never mind my questions. Welcome home. Would you like to get cleaned up while I fix something to eat, or do you want to rest?"

Mrs. Miller looked at her husband, then replied, "I'd like to take a shower?"

"Yes, of course. And I have clothes you can wear," Mrs. Underwood said. She turned to Elm. "Y'all go clean up too."

As Elm hobbled up the stairs, he overheard his dad call the local police. He reported the Miller family had been found.

Later, everyone returned to the table. Elm used a pair of crutches he had from a previous accident. Dinner was on the table.

"Elm, take that filthy cap off your head," his mom said.

"Do you have ice cream?" Jacob asked. "That's what I missed the most."

Mrs. Underwood pulled the ice cream out of the freezer and dipped it into bowls for everyone.

There was a knock at the door.

"Come in," Mrs. Underwood said. Several police and the doctor stood outside.

Everyone greeted the Miller family. The police, along with the Millers, moved into the living room to talk while the doctor checked Elm's foot.

Once the police finished talking to the Millers, the doctor told Mr. Miller to stop by his office tomorrow for a checkup.

That was not the end of the visitors. In a small town, it doesn't take long for word to spread. Many of the townspeople came by with food in hand to welcome the Miller family home and to congratulate the children for finding them.

After a flurry of activities, everyone was exhausted. Elm, Willow, and Randy moved to the living room. Randy settled into a large recliner and fell asleep.

"The portal is closed, isn't it?" Willow asked Elm.

"Yes."

"Do you think we'll get our magic back?"

"Probably not."

Elm thought about everything they had been through. *Are the portals really closed? Will they stay that way?* Maybe he would go back into the woods and check on it. Maybe not. He wasn't sure he ever wanted to go into the forest again.

He petted Sequoia and said. "Never go in the woods again." The dog wagged his tail then curled up beside him.

Elm's eyes grew heavy, and sleep over took his mind. Hearing a gravelly voice, he spun around, he was back in the forest standing in front of the portal. An old hag with stringy, salt and pepper hair that hung down, concealing her face stood on the other side. Crows surrounded her. She was trying to break through the wall.

"This portal may be closed, but we'll find another way." She said to the crows. "Let's check out the wizard's house."

Elm jerked awake. *Was that just a dream? Where's the wizard's house?* He yawned. *I'll check it out in a few days.* Closing his eyes, he fell back asleep.

About the Author

Terry Nolan is thrilled to have her first novel published.

She is originally from Delaware, but now retired and living in Oklahoma with her dog, Ginger.

Made in the USA
Columbia, SC
26 November 2021